The characters and events portrayed in this book are fictitious. Any similarity to real persons, living or dead, is coincidental and not intended by the author.

CONTENTS

Copyright
Chapter One 1
Chapter Two 8
Chapter three 16
Chapter Four 23
Chapter Five 30
Chapter Six 37
Chapter Seven 44
Chapter Eight 53
Chapter nine 60
Chapter Ten 70
Chapter Eleven 80
Chapter Twelve 86
Chapter Thirteen 95

CHAPTER ONE

The car ride was a silent one. But there was nothing silent about the way Joyce's pulse pounded. Even though she had been ecstatic to go on this journey, she did not know if her brother shared the same sentiment.
She was sure they had spoken as much as they could on the phone, but she could not help noting that it would not be the same as meeting each other in person. She hadn't seen her brother in nearly fourteen years. Her heart gave a painful pang at that. It had not been their doing. If she and Larry could have had their way, they would never have been forced apart to grow up without each other.

She tried not to sink into those thoughts but could not help it. She kind of resented her parents for forcing them to grow up like they did. Even though Larry never talked about it, she knew he felt the same way too. After the constant fights, they'd had to experience as kids, they'd also been forced apart because mummy and daddy were much too different to stay together. Splitting the kids had been one thing both had agreed upon and not argued about.

It had torn at Joyce's heart to watch her brother move farther and farther away from her, but she had held on to the promise they had made to each other. They'd never let the distance stop them from continuing to be close. And they'd kept to that promise for thirteen long years. Joyce breathed out through her nose and relaxed into the seat, watching the houses and trees that flew by.

After what seemed like thirty minutes, the car pulled into a gated, traditional-looking home that managed to impress and cause Joyce to shake with nerves at the same time. The magnificent building was a glaring truth about how much different her life was from Larry's. Had their father forced Larry to attend a private school too? She didn't want to think too much about it. Regarding how dissimilar she and Larry could be. Was there even anything they were going to have in common?

While the living conditions with her mother had not been that of a pauper, they had certainly not been this swept-up luxury she was standing in front of right now. A minute later, the door was pushed open, and she expected to see a stern-looking butler usher her in but smiled when Larry bounded over to her and scooped her into his arms. She shrieked at the weird but loving way he greeted her.

He deposited her on the floor after a minute of giving her a bone-crushing hug. "I didn't think you'd follow through with it," he said as if he too could not quite believe that she was standing before him, in flesh and blood.

"Never." She said, her throat clogging up as she stared up at Larry. Even though she had often seen what he looked like when they FaceTimed, nothing had prepared her for how massively handsome her brother was. He was a solid 6.2 as opposed to her 5.8, and she had often considered herself quite tall.

"Dad is waiting in the living room." He said as he grabbed one of her boxes. She smiled gratefully at him and followed him up the stylish pathway. The grass and flowers were pruned to perfection. It caused Joyce to wonder how Larry had felt growing up like this. Father had always loved order and perfection. Mother had been nothing like that. As she continued to look around, she suddenly understood how different both of her parents were.

As they stomped up towards the front door, their breath choppy from hurling the large suitcases Joyce had packed, she felt glad that it was her mother she had ended up with. She loved how laid back she was. She'd raised her, and it was generally how she'd allowed her to live. As she gazed at the pristine walls of the living room of her father's mini-mansion, she was unsure if Larry had been given the luxury of living as she truly did. Carefree. Away from constant order and rules.

"Dad." She said the moment her wondering gaze caught sight of the blonde man who strode towards her.

"Hello, baby," Father said, wrapping her in a hug that was not as bone-crushing as Larry's. "How was the journey?" He asked, dropping his hands and looking as if he didn't quite know what to do with them.

"It has been an eventful one." She said, forcing a smile she hoped had reached her eyes. Standing right here, in front of a man who had sort of abandoned her, felt surreal. And she wasn't going to pretend that the last fifteen years had not happened, that father had not exactly stayed in touch, like Larry had. He had sent the perfunctory birthday and Christmas gifts and congratulated her on each milestone, which was only when she relayed it to him. Father had never really made an effort, not in the way Larry had.

"I'm certain you've had a long journey." He said, skating his fingers lightly across her hair and forcing his hands back down, his gaze darting around, landing on every single item in the luxurious living room except her. She smiled inwardly, not at all surprised at the exchange. This was what distance did. She could tell that her father had missed her, but the distance accumulated through fifteen years of time apart made this encounter awkward.

"Larry will show you to your room." He said, beginning to turn away.

Larry ruffled her hair with a grin and trudged up the stairs. She followed, not looking back to see whether her father was watching her or not.

"That was weird." She commented the moment she was sure they were out of earshot.

"I almost couldn't stand the awkward reconnection," Larry replied. Joyce laughed, her tittering petering out the moment she stepped into the room that was supposedly hers. It felt like she had stepped into one of those rooms often advertised in magazines. She tried not to wince at the splatter of pink across the curtains and sheets.

"What..." Joyce whispered the words dying on her lips.

Larry smirked. "You like it?"

She smiled, hoping it didn't come off as a wince. "Pink isn't exactly my colour."

"Well. Dad might have forgotten that you're no longer that cute blonde little girl in pigtails and missing teeth."

Joyce laughed at that, turning to regard Larry, who stared at her with warmth in his eyes. "I know you're trying to make me feel welcome, but I dunno if this is exactly my scene. Does he even want me here?"

"I think we both know the answer to that. Our workaholic dad in a suit on this blistering afternoon was waiting to welcome you when he could have been in his glass office issuing orders." When Joyce laughed again, Larry continued in a much softer tone, "He's happy to have you. And I am too."

She finally nodded, breathing out

"You know what would shake off your jitters?" Larry asked with a glint in his eye.

"What?"

"Drinks."

Joyce perked up at that, and Larry laughed. "You just turned twenty-one. Still a kid, but it'll do."

Joyce, this time, smacked him in the arm and stood. "I can't say "no" to drinks." The thought of getting out of the house appealed to her more than it should have.

" Great." Larry stood, moving to the door." Freshen up and meet me downstairs in ten."

Joyce grinned and got to her feet, moving towards the ensuite bathroom that looked like she'd need a manual to know how the showers worked. After several failed attempts, she was able to work the shower, deciding on a quick one as opposed to the long stay beneath the spray she wanted.

She fished out skinny jeans out of her suitcase and paired them with a beautiful crop top that displayed her faux belly ring. She grabbed her converse and put them on, blowing out her long blonde hair so that it fell carelessly across her shoulders. She had taken after her dad physically, his replica. It was quite ironical that it was Larry he had favored. She applied minimal makeup and checked herself out in the mirror, loving the image of herself that stared back.

She went downstairs to find Larry already waiting on the patio. He took a quick look at her and grinned. "You clean up nice, kiddo." Joyce simply rolled her eyes at the nickname. She was twenty-, not a kid with a shiner.

"Come on, let's go." He said, striding towards his car. Joyce obediently followed, strapping herself into the passenger seat. "Wait, aren't we going to tell dad?" she asked. Even though she was more than ecstatic to leave the pristine building, she wasn't sure it would be cute to be unmannerly.

"I texted him. He went back to the office. Work emergency." There was a slight bitterness in Larry's voice, which made Joyce wonder if "work emergency" was a frequent thing. Had he even had time to bond properly with Larry as a kid? Or had his work always come first? Just like it was even when he was married to her mother? Deciding not to fixate on the issue, Joyce relaxed into the seat and looked out the window.

A second later, Larry's phone rang. Joyce helpfully connected it to the speaker for him, and he answered. "Sup, dude!"

A deep male voice filtered through the speakers, causing Joyce to jerk slightly forward. The deep baritone of the voice caused something in her chest to stutter. "I just stepped out of the field." The voice replied. Joyce could hear quiet murmurs in the background.

"Good. That means you can join my sister and me for drinks."

"Your sister?" The young man, because yes, it was a man's voice, asked confusedly.

"David," Larry said, almost with an eye roll. "I told you my kid sister was coming for the holidays. Get your butt to Steams and Reems asap." Larry ended the call with a jab and focused on the road.

After a few seconds, he said. "That was my friend, David, I'm sure I've mentioned him a time or two."

Joyce nodded. Larry had mentioned a certain David a couple of times when they FaceTimed. He'd either want to go hang with him or simply help him train. Joyce had never exactly put a face to the name and tried not to think too much about her bodily reaction to the voice.

The rest of the car ride happened in comfortable silence. As Larry pulled into a pleasant-looking bar, he killed the engine and turned to her. "Look, I understand that you might not be on the best of terms with dad, so you can come stay in the apartment I share with David."

"You don't live alone?" Joyce balked.

"Is that a bad thing?" Larry's expression was wary.

"No, no. It isn't. I just didn't think you'd want to stay outside of dad's huge--"

"Joyce." Larry cut in with a slight irritation in his voice. "You know; I feel just as uncomfortable in that huge house as you did an hour ago. The apartment isn't luxurious, but it's home."

Joyce smiled. "I'd love to." She said a broad smile on her face. Larry returned her smile and unbuckled, moving out of the car. Joyce mirrored his movement, stepping out of the car and moving towards the double doors. The bar was scarcely filled, and every patron her eyes landed on seemed to be in their early forties. It made Joyce wonder what they thought of two young adults coming into the bar at-- Joyce brought her wrist up to check the time---4 p.m.

Larry moved to a table that afforded them privacy. The chairs were cushioned, and she relaxed into them, smiling in bliss. The waiter came to take their order. She felt pleased that Larry had allowed her to make her own order. This. Being right here with Larry felt right. She couldn't wait to see what the rest of the holiday had in store for her.

CHAPTER TWO

"They sell food too. Would you like to order something?" Larry asked.

"Not yet." She answered. It felt good to be in a different place. She wondered just how many glasses Larry would let her have. Was he going to continue to be protective just like he had been years ago? When they'd all been one family, and she'd seen him as often as she wanted?

"What are you thinking about?" Larry asked, a curious look in his eyes.

"How pleasant this is." She admitted, looking down at the menu in front of her, making no move to reach for it.

Larry caught onto what she meant because his eyes grew soft. But he didn't say anything else. After another moment where they were each lost in thought, Joyce said softly. "Does Dad ever--I mean; does he have a girlfriend?"

Larry leaned back and looked intently at the menu, but Joyce could tell he wasn't studying it. "When I was still living under his roof, he had a couple of them."

"Whatever happened?"

Larry shrugged. Joyce couldn't tell if he was stalling because he felt he was betraying his father's trust or because he was merely understating the number of women that had walked out of their father's life after mum. "I honestly don't know. I think dad was sensible enough not to let them come home as often as they would have wished to. I didn't really know them, and I was happy not to. But I think it was the same problem."

Joyce feasted her gaze on her brother. "You mean, like with mom?"

Larry hesitated but replied after what seemed like hours. "Yeah, Like with mum." After another minute of absolute silence, it was his turn to struggle to push words past his lips.

"Has mum--did mum ever, um..."

"Mum hasn't dated. Not seriously, anyway. Not since after Dad." She confessed, sparing Larry from cutting his tongue.

Larry looked relieved at the news, and she wondered if he, too, thought that both their parents had not gotten over each other.

"Look, dad may never have--" Larry paused, a slight smile curving his lips as he stared at something past her. She struggled not to crane her head, figuring it was probably his friend.

"Over here, "he called out, waving for good measure. A minute later, Joyce's nose was hit with the enticing cologne of the faceless person's cologne before she made contact with their eyes. Her breath nearly gave out at the electric blue eyes that dipped into hers and switched to her brother.

She stared unblinking at the solidly built and gorgeous person who did the weird handshake boys were fond of with Larry and sat beside him. When Larry began to make introductions, she quickly pulled herself out of her trance and shook hands with the cute brown-headed boy. When his fingers curled around hers, enveloping it, she tried not to visibly gulp at the sparks that shot down her arm.

"It's a pleasure," David said in that deep baritone voice she'd heard spill out of the speaker on their ride here. And this time, the stutter in her heart could not be mistaken. What the he-

"Are you ready to order now?" The waitress said, her eyes fixed on Larry, who looked like he was struggling to keep the blush that had reddened his ears from his cheeks. Was her brother into her?

"Y-yeah. Take their orders, please."

Joyce decided on a simple glass of red wine.

"What about you?" The waitress asked David, who took his time making his order. It gave her the opportunity to study him without looking like a creep. His brown hair was shaggy, his face looked sculpted, and boy, was he toned.

"Coach will have my head if he finds out." He said, shaking his head.

"We won't tell," Larry said, amusement dancing in his eyes. "Will we, Joyce?"

Joyce made a sign of zipping her lips and throwing the key away. "Never."

David's eyes dived right into hers, and she felt transfixed. Never had she seen eyes the color like his. A wild blue. Electric. Riveting.

"Okay." Their playful assurance must have encouraged him because he gave the waitress his order, and Joyce watched as Larry too ordered the same thing, a glass of whiskey.

Conversation after the waitress left was playful. Joyce could not stop watching him as he conversed with Larry, telling him how practice had gone. They moved on to other neutral subjects, the mood was lively, and as she sipped from her glass of red, she could feel a pleasant buzz in her stomach.

Soon enough, the boys were regaling her with tales of college life, and she found herself laughing hard. They appeared to have had more fun in college than she did. Having a studious roommate who did not care too much for parties had been a blessing and a curse. In her first year of college, she had felt like Lilian was a buzz kill, but after seeing how well she had done at the end of the semester, all thanks to her roommate's silent encouragement, she had thanked her lucky stars.

But along the line, she had learned to balance partying and studying. And at that point, it had also been her turn to encourage Lilian, who was an adamant bookworm, to be more... out there. And then, they'd become friends. The parties had not completely sucked, but she doubted she had had fun as much as the boys. Someone snapped their fingers in front of her, and she looked up quickly to realize she had relapsed into silence as her thoughts had taken over.

"Where did you just go to?" Larry asked, a bit of worry in his voice.

"Was thinking about how time really does fly. Feels like I was just a freshman yesterday." She said, tone wistful.

She watched as they both nodded as if they could completely relate. In two months, she was going to write her final paper, and she was going to become a graduate. She had never exactly known what she wanted to do after college. And as she sat there, tracing her fingers over the condensation on her glass, she still did not.

The only thing she was sure of was the fact that she was never going to go back to living with her mom. While the kind woman was the best thing that had ever happened to her, Joyce wanted to venture out on her own. Live alone. Make her own decisions. Making mistakes and learning from them, and she had a feeling her mother had also been holding back on dating until she moved out. Not that she was ever going to come out and say it.

"Would you like another drink?"

Joyce's eyes were locked on David's, who looked at her questioningly. She looked down to realize her glass of wine was down to its bottom. "I would love one. Thanks." She said, ignoring the light flutter at the realization that David was sort of studying her.

As David signaled the waitress, who sauntered over, Larry's phone rang. Joyce watched him, biting her bottom lips in worry when he began to frown but continued to nod to questions the caller was probably asking as if the caller could see him.

Putting the phone down with a sigh, Larry turned apologetic eyes on her. That was my boss."

Joyce knew what was coming. And she couldn't even quell the feelings of disappointment that swamped her stomach." We need to go, right?"

"You don't have to be anywhere, just me." Larry started. Maybe he had seen the look of disappointment in her eyes. "You could stay and get your second drink. David will stay with you, take you home right after."

At the mention of David, that flutter in her stomach started again, nearly tempting her to place a hand against her stomach. She smiled at her brother. "It's fine, and I'd hate to make him feel put out." Her stomach felt queasy at the thought of going back to the big house.

"I meant it when I said you could stay at ours." Larry looked intensely at her as if daring her to argue again.

Joyce's eyes lit up, and a relieved smile took up her entire face. She could feel David's eyes watching her out of the corner of her eyes, and as a blush coated her cheeks, she hoped they would surmise it to feelings of excitement. "That'd be great."

"Good. I'll call you as soon as I'm done at the office." Larry said, getting up and moving quickly out of the bar. David and Joyce fell into silence at Larry's departure, both unsure at first what to talk about. Joyce could tell that David was watching her but could not bring herself to look up and into his eyes. She didn't want to risk having him find out the sort of effect his presence was having on her.

The silence was tense. And Joyce, for the life of her, did not know how to break it. Maybe she could attempt it if she could look into his eyes without feeling star struck. Thankfully, the waitress arrived with her second glass, and she held it as if her life depended on it, taking a long sip that caused David's eyes to widen.

"Hey, slow down," he chuckled.

She snorted a laugh, another blush coating her cheeks at the strange sound. "Sorry, dunno why I'm nervous."

David gave a low laugh that caused her pulse to hammer a bit harder. "When I walked in here and met your eyes, I got nervous too."

Joyce found that hard to believe, not with the way he'd held himself and looked into her eyes with confidence. "Really?" She questioned her doubtfully. "Are you simply trying to make me feel better?"

"No, I'm not. Being honest. You are beautiful." At that point, he looked up, and their gazes locked. Joyce's heart hammered with a vengeance, a corresponding pulse starting between her thighs. David's eyes had grown dark with desire, and Joyce felt an insurmountable need to reach out a hand and brush his brown curls.

She was forced to watch as David's gaze shifted between her eyes and lips, desire apparent in his gleaming orbs. She watched him and then smiled. "You're a footballer, huh?"

"You're correct." He said, shifting slightly in his seat. Joyce grinned to herself. She wanted David. The last time someone had caught her eye like this was her previous boyfriend in her third year. He had turned out to be a dickhead, and she had dumped him without a second thought. As she gazed at David, she knew what she wanted. And now, away from the watchful eyes of her brother, she could put her feminine wiles to good use.

"What about you?"

Joyce gazed at him beneath her lashes and then leaned back,

watching as his eyes followed her movements. "Are you asking if I'm a player?" She had made her voice low, dropping one hand on the cushion she leaned on, a deliberate move that caused her white crop top to heave up, exposing her toned stomach.

David seemed to be having a problem swallowing because he made a strangled sound and began to cough hard, face reddening.

"Are you alright?" She asked, dropping her hands to his shoulder, marveling at the toned flesh that flexed beneath her hands.

"I'm fine." He said, his slightly stinging eyes meeting hers. Joyce reluctantly dropped her hands and sipped again from her glass, giving David time to regain his composure.

When he did, he looked up at her with burning eyes. "I think you know what you're doing to me."

"Do I?" She asked in a dull tone of voice that did not quite match the fire in her eyes.

He looked at him then and, with slow, practiced speed, skirted his fingers along the skin of her arm. Her shiver was unmistaken, and he smiled in a self-absorbed way that she found devastatingly cute. They gazed at each other for what appeared to be hours.

"We should head out." He said, pushing out a few dollar notes and dropping them on the desk. Joyce looked out to realize it had fallen dark. As he stood, Joyce followed suit, moving with him out of the door. As his shoulder brushed against hers by the door, his hands moving to her lower back, caressing the exposed skin there, another shiver racked her body. The throbbing in her legs became incessant, and as they buckled into his sports car, she knew how she wanted the night to end.

CHAPTER THREE

The car ride was filled with sexual tension, and it didn't help that David kept adjusting, maybe in hopes of hiding his growing bulge. Joyce's own desire was spiking to greater heights. It had been so long, too long, since she had had an instant attraction to someone. Whatever this was with David needed to be followed through. She wanted to explore whatever this was, to find out what made the player tick.
When David adjusted for the third time in ten minutes, she chuckled. "Are you uncomfortable?" She asked as if she did not know what he was going through, as if the same throbbing that kept his thighs from closing did not plague hers.

"I don't know how to answer that question."

"Well. I think I might have an idea of what you might be going through." Her tone, which she had intended to be low and mocking, came out breathy, making her arousal obvious to David, who glanced quickly at her before focusing back on the road.

"I can't wait." She began when her thighs began to burn with an irrepressible need.

"What?" David croaked, his hands on the steering wheel shaking slightly.

"Have you had too much to drink?" She asked, panic slithering through her, momentarily obliterating her sexual desires.

"God, no." "It was just one glass, and I hadn't even gotten around to finishing it. Trust me; I'm stone-cold sober."

She nodded. "Hold onto that wheel like your life depends on it because you'll need it." With that, she slipped her hands through her roomy crop top, grabbing both her tits and moaning delightfully at the feel of warm hands on them.

"What the f-fuck?" She heard David splutter beside her. She grinned to herself and continued. This show was as much for him as it was for her. She needed this release, craved it. Who was to say they wouldn't meet Larry at the apartment when they got back? She wouldn't be able to do anything then. This was her chance, her time. And she was going to make the best of it.

"Are you going to... right here?" David asked, his Adam Apple bobbing up and down.

"Yes. I should wait." She responded, her voice tinged with arousal. "I can't."

"Oh fuck..."

"What? You've never watched a woman come?"

David made a strangled noise like he was dying, and Joyce laughed. It was funny because merely an hour ago, she had been the one feeling tongue-tied. Her heart had been producing jitters, making her too aware of the young man who had sat opposite her. Now that she had taken carnal matters into her own hands, the table had seemed to turn a solid 360 and entirely in her favour.

When David failed to answer, Joyce pinched her nipples and moaned at the jolt of pleasure that shot straight through her. "Have you never watched a woman come?" She asked yet again, her eyes now closed, her mouth slightly open to take in puffs of air.

"I mean, I've had several girlfriends who have, uh, h-have--"

"Would you like to watch me come, David?"

"This time, David's response was a strangled groan. I'm so turned on right now that I can't even see straight."

"Good. It means you're as ready for me as I am for you."

"Oh fuck." David gripped the steering wheel tighter. He had been driving by sheer reflex. His eyes had gone hazy with arousal; his hands, which continued to clutch the steering wheel for dear life, felt numb.

When Joyce's hands dropped to her stomach, pushing at the waistband of her jeans, David cursed. Joyce ignored his expletives, her hands feverishly seeking the wealth of wetness between her thighs.

A second later, she pried her eyes open. "Why have we stopped?" She asked David, who had parked the car and turned to her with burning eyes. "You could get a ticket for packing unlawfully."

"I do not care."

"Well, I do."

"I can't continue to drive. Not in this condition," he explained, his eyes skittering away and back to her. "What you're doing is enough to kill us both."

"Well, that wasn't my plan."

"What was?" He asked desperately as if he needed some sort of consent to hurl her into the backseat of his car and have his devious way with her.

"Well, my plan, which I planned to not disclose, seems to have worked out perfectly. I, for one, have you where I want you." She said, eyes blazing with lust, her lips parted.

David closed his eyes briefly, and when he opened them, Joyce knew what was coming next. One second, she was on her side of the car; the next, she was beneath David, kissing him back with a reckless passion that caused a tight moan to wrestle up her throat.

David appeared to have overcome his earlier bumble and mumble because he kissed her with the assurance of someone who knew what they wanted. He coaxed her lips open, plunging his tongue into her mouth with a vengeance that caused her heart to soar. Her sweet little act had managed to rile him up just like she had wanted, and now she found herself at his mercy, getting everything he was giving. His tongue stroked in and out of her mouth, his searching fingers that had moved to her breast, pinching the nipples through her bra almost exactly as she had done to herself minutes before.

She arched into him, moaning his name breathily. David plucked yet again at the turgid nipples, tearing another moan out of her. His fingers searched lower, his mouth never leaving hers. She tried not to cry out when that hot mouth descended lower, biting at the skin of her neck slightly and then suiting the slight sting with kisses. "You are very naughty; you know that?" He whispered against the shell of her ear, nipping her lobe slightly.

Joyce's only response was a pleasurable murmur and her hips canting upwards, searching for any sort of friction that would propel her into her orgasm that was dancing a little out of reach.

"Answer me," he whispered fiercely, his hands cupping her through her jeans a bit forcefully, causing the hard fabric to jab her clit, an action that caused bolts upon bolts of pleasure to arc through her, nearly tearing a scream out of her. "You've been a naughty little girl, haven't you?"

"Yes." She found herself answering. She had been naughty too. And needed him to want her as much as she wanted him. And that had seemed to work, maybe a little too much, judging from how hard David's member was pressed against her stomach.

"You know what happens to naughty girls, don't you?"

She nodded rigorously. But when his lustful eyes glared, she scrambled to reply verbally. "Yes."

"What?" He asked, his hands casually moving to the button of her jeans, snapping it open.

"Oh my God!" She cried out when David's fingers combed through her wet slit. She tried to part her legs wider, to create friction, but his caresses were light, almost feather-like.

"David," she said in a voice she didn't recognize as her own. "I need to come."

"You do?" He asked, his fingers moving lower, gathering her wetness and rubbing it over her nub.

"Y-yes, o-please. Please, David." She found herself begging when the fire beneath her legs spiraled to great heights.

With a groan, David slipped a finger into her tight wet core and began to move in and out. A moan fell from her lips, and her eyes rolled back at the sensations that swirled inside of her, ran through her blood scream, and tightened her stomach.

"You're so wet," David observed in a desire-roughened voice.

"All your fault," she muttered, gripping him tighter, moving her hips in tandem with his fingers. She moaned when his fingers brushed against a spot that sent shudders through her. "I'm so close... D-don't stop. Please..."

"Never." He answered, ramping up his movements, taking her higher and higher. The moment her walls tightened around his fingers, the phone blared out loudly, startling them both. David yanked his hands away from her and grabbed the phone, his shoulder tensing. Joyce watched him, already guessing who was at the other end of the line.

"Hey, Larry. We are just on our way."

She couldn't make out what her brother was saying. But David had a concentrated look on his face as he moved further away from her, back to the driver's seat. With one hand, he began to buckle himself in. "That's good. See you later." He hung up and quickly put the car in drive.

Without throwing a glance her way, David said. "Larry would be back in an hour. I can make it home in ten minutes."

"And then what?"

"And then, we make the most of forty minutes." He answered simply, continuing the drive home.

*****

Their home, Joyce noted, was simple but well furnished. There was no time to give her a tour, though; they had managed to make it home in eight minutes, and at this point, every second mattered.

David wasted no time in dragging her to his room. The moment the door closed, he backed her against it and started to plant kisses on her neck. This time, there was no stopping the uncontrollable way he touched her. He ripped her clothes off in seconds, branding her skin with his lips.

Her orgasm, which had been seconds away from crashing on her in the car, was back with a vengeance, arcing through her body, making her skin hot. She gripped his bicep and arched, her eyes slipping close to the sensations that raced through her body.

"There's so much I want to do for you. But there's little time." He whispered against her lips, his hands traveling to the apex of her thighs.

"Yes." She whispered. But when his fingers met the wetness that had seemed to multiply, she groaned. "Don't leave me halfway again." She warned.

David's only response was the insertion of two digits inside of her.

"Oh fuck." She screamed, her legs parting wider to accommodate the movement of his fingers. David's thrust inside of her was relentless, and within moments, he had propelled her into a mind-numbing orgasm that turned her legs jelly.

She would have crumbled to the ground if not for his arms that had wrapped around her midsection, holding her steady. When she could catch her breath, David hurled her effortlessly up and moved towards the large bed in the corner of the room. The orgasm that had just rippled through her should have sated her, but rather, she felt like David had merely given her a prelude to the real thing.

She found herself tearing through his clothes, needing his naked skin against hers. She shucked down her trousers in haste, assisting him to do the same. A minute later, their bodies came together, skin slinking against skin. Joyce moaned at the bronzed skin against hers. It was a bit overwhelming.

She parted her legs in silent invitation, growling when David rather contented himself with kissing her into oblivion. She found herself responding, her desires rekindled to frightening proportions. David pampered her with his tongue and fingers until she sobbed and begged. When he finally slipped into her, she was so ready that her moisture practically coated her inner thighs, making them slick.

David moved in and out of her, every thrust tearing a moan out of her. It was all too much, the deft way David handled her body, angling just right so that his cock brushed against a part inside of her that caused a strangled moan to spill out of her. Just when she thought she could not take more of the onslaught, David's fingers slipped between them, flicking her clit in tandem with his thrusts, pushing her over the precipice. She came with a tight scream, her back arching so high she nearly toppled David over.

David let himself ride the crest with her, spilling his loads into her and collapsing into her when they rode the last waves. He rolled off of her and hastily slipped into his pants.

Joyce looked blearily at him. "Your brother could be back any second." He explained.

Joyce nodded. "Give me a minute," she said, her eyes slipping closed, and she fell into a fitful slumber.

CHAPTER FOUR

It took Joyce several moments to recall why she was in a strange bed. But that was after panicking for a second that she had done something untoward, which had, in fact, been what she had. As she scrambled out of her bed with the sheets wrapped protectively around her, she searched around for her clothes, finding her pants and top at the door, ignoring the headache that pounded at the back of her skull.

It was the constant price she had to pay for drinking. And it was quite hilarious that despite the after-effects of alcohol, it didn't stop her from drinking.

Her face flamed at the hazy memory of being slammed against the door, her outfit hastily taken off of her. When her mind went back to the car ride and the wanton way she had behaved, her whole face pinked. Even though she had had one-night stands in the past, she had never done anything so obscene. She guessed the alcohol had given her the bravery to carry out all of those.

She feared what David would think of her now, sober and hungover. She slipped into her old clothes, grimacing slightly at the wrinkles. There was nothing she could do about it, and it wasn't like she had packed extra, so she had to make do.

When she heard voices outside thc room, she panicked. When had her brother returned? Had he found her sprawled in his best friend's bed naked? She sure as hell hoped not. That would be scandalous, and she doubted she would ever face her brother if that had happened.

She moved into the ensuite bathroom, noting how organized everything was. Every damn thing had its own place, and nothing was out of place. Not even a stray hair. The pristine bathroom reminded her of her father's home. Ignoring the obvious sign of OCD, she did her business and brushed out her hair with the little comb she found placed perfectly in its little holder. Like she said, every single item in here had its own place.

She moved out, squaring her shoulders, ready to meet her brother. She found the duo in the kitchen, with cups of coffee in hand. She groaned at the sweet scent of coffee that drifted into her nose, moving straight to the kettle to pour herself a cup.

"Good morning to you too, little sister."

"I can't talk." She croaked. "Hungover."

Larry's laughter sounded like he'd parted her ears and guffawed right into her ear drum. She winced, almost clutching her ears at the intense throbbing the loud sound wrought. David must have caught onto the movement because he jabbed her brother in the ribs and told him to quiet down.

David, she observed out of the corner of her eyes, was dressed in shorts and a muscled shirt that did nothing to hide his impressive biceps. She recalled those hands wrapped around her, hurling her up, throwing her onto the bed. She might have been drunk, but she could remember every single detail of last night.

She took the coffee to the kitchen island, making herself comfortable on the last chair, which was thankfully close to Larry's. She wasn't sure she could bear the awkwardness of trying to push through a conversation with David, not when he had been inside of her hours ago.

"How was last night?"

Joyce nearly choked on her first sip of coffee but ended up spilling the content all over the kitchen island. "Sorry," she apologized when she had managed to stop coughing.

"Are you alright?" Larry asked concernedly, ignoring the mess she had made on the kitchen island.

"I'm fine. My brain isn't fully awake, I guess."

"How many glasses did you have?" Larry asked, a frown crossing his features as he glanced at David, who had managed to remain silent and calm through the short debacle.

"Two glasses."

"Oh." Larry grinned. "You're a lightweight."

She should have argued that. But she simply rolled her eyes and stood, grabbing a dishrag David had pointed her to clean up the mess on the island. She tried to ignore the tight frown that had crossed David's features at the mess. She could not help but notice the way he had averted his gaze as if the sight of the slight mess was bothersome. He reminded her so much of her dad that it was ridiculous. She wondered how Larry and he were friends. It was more than obvious that her brother was nothing like that.

When she climbed back up onto the stool, Larry's face had grown more serious. She angled her body towards his, ignoring the way David gazed at her fingers as if she had dabbled them in mud, even though she had washed right after drying out the rag. Should she use hand sanitizer too?

"For the rest of the week, Dad wants you to stay at the mansion," Larry said.

Joyce could not hide her frown. "Why?"

"He wants to bond with you. And apparently, he wants us to get to know his wife-to-be."

"What?" Joyce spluttered. "A what?"

Larry shook his head, glancing at David, who appeared to be very focused on his phone. Larry was definitely going to give her the full scoop later.

"What do you mean by 'us'?"

"I'll have to come stay at the mansion. at least for the duration of your stay in California."

Joyce nodded. "At least you'll be there."

"We leave today," Larry informed her ruefully.

This time, Larry's words managed to snag David's attention because he glanced up quickly, his eyes meeting hers. His expression was direct, but she didn't know how to read it. Was he glad to be rid of her? Unhappy that she was leaving so quickly? Had he wished for their little tryst to continue?

She was the first to look away, focusing on Larry, who appeared to peer deep into his cup of coffee as if the swirly brown liquid held all the answers to his questions.

"I can't wait to see the kind of woman my dad has finally decided to settle with." She thought aloud.

"Me too."

When David abruptly stood and moved towards the direction of his room, Joyce was momentarily distracted by the toned, sturdy legs that flexed with each step he took. There was something sexy about the way he strode, a bit casually as if he had all the time in the world.

The shorts were molded against his body, emphasizing his taut ass. She could not help but remember smoothing her fingers across faultless flesh as he had continuously plunged into her. She could feel a prickling sensation between her thighs that was all too familiar. Dragging her eyes away from the player's stunning ass, Joyce was shocked to find her brother's eyes on her, openly judging her. Her cheeks reddened, and her gaze dipped to her coffee, which she had suddenly found an immeasurable interest in. "Do you fancy Dave?"

"Fancy?" She scoffed. "Is this the nineties?"

"Do you have the hots for my friend?" Larry rephrased, his eyes never leaving her face.

Joyce's face reddened further at her brother's choice of words. The truth was that David was hot as hell and had not minded their little rendezvous last night, and if she was completely honest with herself, she didn't mind a repeat either. She wondered how to answer his question without giving her lustful thoughts away.

"You should know," her brother continued when it became evident she was going to give his question no answer. "Dave isn't really in the market for a relationship. And I would hate to see my little sister frolic with him."

"Larry, chill. I have no plans to shag your friend." Larry flinched at her words, and she had the decency to look embarrassed but forged on anyways. "I am only going to spend two weeks here. There is no sense in starting something that is bound to come to an inevitable end."

Her words must have been convincing enough because, Larry said, with a sigh of obvious relief. "Good."

She nudged his shoulders, and he turned to face her with a smile. "What?" He asked. "I'm just happy I don't have to give you all the pep talk and shit. It's weird enough that I caught you eyefucking him."

Joyce allowed her head to fall onto the kitchen island with a thump. "Oh my God. Really, Larry?"

Her brother's only response was a loud chuckle before he clambered off the seat and strode towards his own room. "We have to pack. Dad expects us home before noon anyway."

Joyce nodded but made no move to get up. She needed her cup of coffee and a little bit of quiet to ensure her skull wasn't about to fuck her over. And then mentally prepare herself to be civil to her father and whoever he had decided to spend the rest of his life with.

It was going to be an interesting two weeks.

******

Joyce sat with her brother and tried to pretend she hadn't felt hurt that she hadn't had time to say goodbye to David. It wasn't like she had been hoping to get his number and try to keep in touch or anything absurd like that. Whatever buttery feelings had tried to rear their heads had flailed and died the moment she had noticed the player's mild OCD. She was going to consider it mild because she didn't know him well enough to make final judgements. Maybe he wasn't as terrible as she thought. Dad had loved to arrange his ties according to their colors. Maybe he was worse.

She shivered at the thought and looked out the window. Larry had put on a song to fill the silence, which had made Joyce figure that he, too, needed time to think. Their father's sudden wedding intention was bizarre. She could tell that the sudden news had caught Larry off guard too.

She wondered how she would react if her mother popped out to announce her intention to remarry. She wouldn't take it sitting down; that much was certain. She figured Larry felt that way too. He felt a sense of betrayal. Whoever the woman was, though, she hoped she was the real deal. It would be scandalous to have two failed marriages.

Twenty minutes later, Larry was pulling into the familiar driveway and riding up to what looked like a swanky garage, remotely controlled. She moved out as soon as he parked and looked around. She was surprised to discover the space was vast enough to accommodate several other cars. Her father had always pretty much been stuffed up. It was one of the reasons he had agreed for her mother to have the house in the divorce settlement, as well as the juicy figure the court had also declared.

Joyce waited until Larry stepped out and moved towards her so that they could move into the mansion together. With growing trepidation, they both mounted the steps in unison and stepped into the lavishly decorated living room that had not a speck of dust in place. Her eyes swing towards the spotless white couch that sat her father and a young woman that looked--wait, what? That was the woman her father was hoping to marry?

"Joyce, darling." Her father called out in an enthusiastic voice as if he was trying to compensate for something, moving towards them with the woman in tow. Joyce could not keep the shock from her face. The woman couldn't have been older than her own twenty-two years! What was her father thinking? Or had he even thought at all?

"Did you have a great time yesterday? David informed me you'd both been out for drinks."

She nodded dumbly, her eyes moving towards Larry, who practically shook with rage, but managed to hold himself together.

"That's good." Her father responded with a smile as if this meeting was normal. As if anything about this moment was normal. "I wanted you to meet my fiancée, Emily. I know this is sudden and quite...unexpected but--

" It really is." Larry cut in, his voice acidic." I never even met her until now."

" That's because I met her not too long ago myself," their father replied, eyes switching towards Emily, who had a sweet smile plastered on her face. Joyce could not tell if she was faking it. Was the girl even out of college? She doubted she even wanted to know.

" We can have lunch. Discuss more at the table," her father said when the sudden silence became deafening. Joyce nodded and moved towards the dining room.

What the hell was going on with her father? And could this visit get any more bizarre?

CHAPTER FIVE

Lunch consisted of fajitas with a marinated grilled skirt steak served in a wheat flour tortilla. Joyce would have enjoyed it immensely, except that the tension was so palpable at the table that she could practically cut it with a knife. She had quickly taken a seat beside Larry, who looked like he was seconds away from bursting into a thousand billion pieces. Joyce was hoping he could hold out being civil long enough for the lunch to be over. She didn't think any good could come from slapping her father's infant wife across the face.

"So," Larry began, in a voice that was surprisingly quiet, cut with undercurrents of anger that caused everyone at the table to momentarily drop their spoons. "Emily, right?"

Joyce, who had vowed not to look in the woman's general direction, found herself looking up, watching her reaction. Emily seemed like she was sensible enough to sense the tension in the room. Her shoulders appeared tense but other than that, she appeared surprisingly calm with that same stupid smile plastered on her face.

"Did you attend college here?"

Emily thought for a moment and then answered. "Actually, I went to school in London. Studied accounting and financial management. I came here to California to intern. Which I had happened to do in your father's company." She glanced at her father, and the fond look she dashed his way could not be mistaken. On the other hand, he seemed to be concentrating very hard on his fajitas. Joyce guessed he knew that it was only normal to get to know his wife, right? As if that was not what this whole vacation was about.

"When did you come to California?" Larry asked, making no attempt to sound conversational. These were questions jabbed at her with the aim of getting to know what the hell the strange girl wanted.

"A little over seven months ago."

"When did you graduate from college?" Their father's spoon clattered to the table, but Larry never took his eyes off Emily, who seemed to be handling herself well.

"Actually, I graduated a year ago."

"How old are you?"

Emily must have been expecting the question because she replied easily with a smile. "I'm 24. I'll be twenty-five in three months."

Joyce tsked. Okay, so Emily was much older than they thought, which was a relief, of course. She could see that Larry thought the same thing because his fingers dropped his spoon with a little less clatter and his deep scowl seemed to have receded at least a little. Emily smiled and said, Conversationally. "I know I've always looked younger than I am. I had professors who constantly questioned what I did in the classes on their first day." She shook her head as if she had found the whole ordeal funny, the same way she was probably finding this whole episode or was probably going to afterward.

" I know this is wild and unexpected, but I actually love your father." This time, Joyce caught movement beneath the table and knew they were holding hands. Anger, white and searing, coursed through her body.

"Love?" She sneered, surprised that she was actually the one who could not control herself. "What do you know about loving a man old enough to be your father?"

"Joyce!" Larry called in a tone that managed to sound both warning and amazed at the same time. Probably because he had never seen her mad. That was to be expected, seeing as the only time they ever got to bond was when they stared at each other through the web cam on their laptops.

"Tell me." She snarled. "What do you know about it? Or are you simply finding a weak old man who's starved himself of love and emotional connection long enough to not be able to tell the difference?"

"Joyce, that's enough." Her father's voice rang out, loud and authoritative. She had never had her father use that tone of voice on her, and it shocked her into silence. And she found the herself plopping back onto the chair in a daze. "Is this why you invited me over? After thirteen years of wanting nothing to do with me, you suddenly developed a weird interest in my affairs and wanted father-daughter bonding time to tell me that you'd moved on to a woman my age."

"Emily is not your age, Joyce." He answered regret tinged in his voice. But at what? Joyce could not tell. Was he regretting his little outburst or this entire sordid affair? She could just picture her mother's face at the news that her father was getting married to a woman closer to her own age than hers. Joyce covered her face with her hands and tried to hold in the sob that threatened to spill. There was no way she was going to cry for them. There was no way she was going to do that.

"I know how this may seem." Emily began. And this time, there was no sunny smile etched on her face, thank God. Because Joyce was unsure she would have been able to resist leaning over and stabbing the woman's symmetrical features with a fork. "But your dad and I truly love each other. Age is just a number. It isn't taken into consideration, when it comes to love. Your father and I tried to ignore our feelings and tried to stay friends. It didn't work. I don't care about Collin's money; I just want to be with him."

She looked sincere enough that for almost a second, Joyce nearly believed her. She also found that she wanted to, but she didn't think she could handle having a stepmother who was closer to her age than her mother's, who would eventually turn out to be a good digger.

"So, when is the wedding?"

"Oh, no. We haven't decided yet." Emily admitted it with a smile. Her father, who had been concentrating on his meal, gave her a fond look.

"We were hoping we could get you guys to, you know, get to know her well. Hang out" he said, a hopeful look on his face.

"Hang out?" Joyce spat and saw her father look quickly away. At least he was aware of how bizarre that sounded.

"So, now that you've brought Larry and me to the mansion, what do you expect us to do? Hang out with your wife to be? Will she braid my hair and tell childhood stories?"

"Joyce. You don't have to make this harder than it is."

"It was hard enough when you left mom and me." She yelled, her eyes stinging with tears. Afraid there were going to fall, Joyce quickly rounded the table and dashed up the steps without another word. She was certain that if she even managed to work the words past her throat, the only thing she was going to push through would be tears.

She was glad no one had come after her. And so, she went straight to the room Larry had shown her to yesterday. Dad must have called in someone because the house seemed cleaned, her boxes put away. Whoever had done it, she was utterly grateful to them. It was probably the housekeeper or something. She made a mental note to thank them whenever she saw them and fell onto the bed.

She stared up at the ceiling, trying to imagine that this truly was her life. A twenty-four-year-old woman married to a man in his early fifties? What the hell? What the absolute hell? Should there not be a law against that? A law ensuring that people did not go about doing the oddest things?

She shook her head. At least her anger had returned, and she was no longer on the verge of tears. Their father had never cared about her, not on a deep level anyway. Not as he should have. And she hated that it hurt deeper than she had expected it to. He knew that the little holiday he had proposed wasn't to spend as much time as he could with her. He simply wanted to introduce his little wife. Joyce was startled when her phone blared out the obnoxious ring tone she used and quickly grabbed it out of her pack pocket, a little smile curving her lips at the displayed name.

"Hey."

"God, I was half afraid you were lying in a ditch somewhere. Why the hell did you not call me to share your arrival?"

"Sorry. I, uh," Joyce apologized to her roommate and best friend. "I just sort of ran into really bizarre stuff here."

"Really? Like what?" Lilian asked. "A haunted house with several vaults, and you get to spend the rest of your vacation solving puzzles? Sounds like fun."

Joyce simply rolled her eyes. but answered anyway. "I'd have been delighted to come to a haunted home and puzzled vaults. I'm not sure it would have given me the sort of instant migraine this has." Her last words were a low murmur.

There was a pause at the other end of the line. And then Lilian said, "Are you alright?"

"As fine as I can be."

"That's code for hell's about to break loose. Come on, tell me. Is it something I can help with? Do you need me to call and lie about failing a course and the need for the urgency of your return to campus?"

"What?"

"Sorry. It's the only plausible reason I can think of at the moment. But really, do you need me there? You sound distressed."

"That's because I am. Dad is getting married."

"Uh," Lillian said, a confused tilt in her tone. "That's, um, great?"

"No. It's absolutely not. This girl is closer to my age than his."

This time, it was Lilian's turn to balk. "What?"

"Yes," Joyce said, feeling slightly smug at the note of shock in her friend's voice. "This girl," because, yes, Emily was still a girl who knew next to nothing about marriage. "I don't know what they're doing; it looks like child's play. It's all so surreal. And Dad expects us to spend time with her."

"Hold up," Lilian said. "Your dad invited you over to bond with his wife, who's like, half his age?"

Joyce grinned. Lillian had always been a smart one, which was the reason they were even friends in the first place. "You're spot on."

"And your brother?"

"He's got an apartment he shares with his friend. But he's expected to bond with the young wife too. So we are all here. It's so fucked up. I can't believe this is my life. This only happens in sitcoms."

"You mean romcoms?"

"Whatever." Joyce rolled her eyes. "I just don't want to do any bonding. Not with her, anyways. I'd thought he really missed me. That he truly wanted to catch up. I didn't know there was a catch for him to me coming here."

"Maybe he does want to spend time with you."

"Like hell he does." Joyce's tone was dark, and her face had twisted into a scowl.

"How would your mum feel about this?" Lillian, always so insightful, asked.

Joyce gulped. In all this, she hadn't even thought about what her mum's reaction would be. Losing her husband to a woman half her age? A woman no older than her own daughter? Joyce gritted her teeth until her gums hurt. "I'd hate to be the one to break the news to her," she said, turning on her stomach and staring gloomily at the curtain.

Lilian's tone was slightly cautious when she said it. "If they truly love each other and want to be together for genuine reasons, it'd be unfair for anyone to stand in the way of that."

"What?" Joyce barked.

"I'm just saying your father deserves to remarry. To be happy. He's stayed unmarried long enough."

Joyce paused, mulling it over. She figured she could forgive him for being so patient. At the very least, he hadn't bolted into a woman's arms the moment they both signed the papers.

"We will see how it goes. If Emily is a two-timing bitch whose intent is to dig her knuckles into my dad's--"

"We'd hunt her down and gut her. I'll even help you hide the body." Lilian cut in dryly.

Joyce grinned at that. "That sounds like a plan."

"Good. Be home soon. Okay?"

Joyce laughed, her mood lightening. "Yes, mum."

"Good."

"And Joyce?"

"Yeah?"

"I'm not your goddamn mum." Joyce's only response was more laughter as Lilian hung up. As she dropped the phone and watched it bounce, she was glad that she had a great friend.

CHAPTER SIX

Joyce was awakened by a light tap on her door. She stared around blearily, wondering what the heck she was doing in a room that looked like it was designed for a twelve-year-old. And then, the memories returned. The vacation. Dad. A new wife. The last thought left a bitter taste in her mouth, and she swallowed.

Another knock came again, and this time, she pushed out of bed and moved towards the door, with the assumption that it'd be Larry. Her father would not enter her room, talk to her, or try to persuade her that a barely out of adolescence woman was suitable for marriage. At the thought, a full throbbing in her skull began again, and she sighed, pulling the door open and coming face to face with a nice-looking Emily.

"What do you want?" Joyce knew she sounded like a petulant teenager. But she didn't care. She wasn't going to play nice. No.

Emily, however, seemed unswerving and still managed to flash a smile that made her frown harder. "I wanted to inform you of dinner."

"I'm not hungry," she returned in a clipped tone, taking a step back so she could slam the door in her perfect face. Of course, her dad had to go for a woman who looked like she was meant for the runway. She refused to allow the woman's obvious beauty to eat away at her self-esteem.

Emily, however, had hard-sharp reflexes and had shot out an arm to block the door. Joyce looked at her in surprise. But she only smiled again. "You can have yours here. If you do not want to join your dad and me."

Joyce rolled her eyes. What card was she playing at? Was she trying to win her over? Was she that desperate? Even though it was on the tip of her tongue to ask that, Joyce knew it would be really low of her to do so, so she instead clucked her tongue, took a deep breath, and said. "I would not like for you to bring my meal to me, Emily."

For the first time, Joyce saw a look of hurt cross the woman's features and didn't know whether to feel elated or bad. But what she hated the most was her stupid brain for considering the woman's feelings in the first place.

"We are having pizza." Emily, who had seemed to get over her mean words, said, "And your father mentioned the toppings are your favourite."

Joyce swallowed and tried not to salivate at the thought of the delectable delight. She loved pizza; who didn't? Emily must have seen her momentary look of hunger because she dived in for the kill immediately." You don't have to have me bring it to you. You can come get it yourself, if you're afraid I might poison you."

"Of course, there's a lot you stand to gain if you do that." Joyce snapped her attitude back.

Emily simply shook her head and began to move downstairs. Joyce didn't know whether to haul her back by the scruff of her neck and yell in her face or give her an apology for how bitchy she'd acted. She hated that her feelings were everywhere. It was frustrating not to know what the woman wanted.

Joyce returned to her room just in time to hear her phone ring. She picked it up, and her heart clenched at the caller ID.

"Hello, mom." She gave a greeting in a voice that was far too cheerful.

"Hello, baby girl." Her mother's greeting was drawn out, pointing to her confusion at Joyce's chirpiness. "Are you having the time of your life?"

"Absolutely." She answered earnestly. Even though she was lying through her teeth, she couldn't bring herself to tell her the real state of things. She didn't think she could bear to hear the pain in her mother's voice without wanting to throttle Emily. And also, she had had the time of her life last night when David had literally fucked her brains out, but she guessed that was news her mother was better off not knowing.

"That's great. H-how's your brother?" She asked hesitantly.

"He's alright. We hung out yesterday." She had kept in touch with her son as much as she had. But she guessed it wasn't enough. She knew her mother missed Larry immensely.

"That's good to hear." They talked a lot more about mundane things, and ten minutes later, they were saying their goodbyes. Joyce threw her phonc on the bed and grabbed her stomach when it growled loudly. Glaring at the door, she moved towards it. As much as she hated Emily right now, skipping dinner wasn't going to happen.

She went downstairs towards the kitchen to the murmur of voices. There was a giggle. As Joyce moved to the open door, she caught sight of Emily feeding her father a slice of pizza. She looked awfully happy doing it; her face practically glowed with mirth. Her heart clenched at the sight. Her gaze drifted to her father, who playfully chased her fingers with his mouth, making her giggle even louder. He was still in his slacks and shirt but had given up the tuxedo.

Even in his office attire, he was the most relaxed she had seen him. When her father suddenly snaked an arm around Emily and pulled her to himself, Joyce decided she had had enough of the PDA and, trying not to gag, cleared her throat. Hard. And was quite satisfied to see them jump apart with guilt written on their faces.

She strolled into the cooking area as if she hadn't stood five minutes to watch them and grabbed a plate, dumping two slices of pizza on it. When she rummaged through the fridge for something to drink, she didn't look at either of them. The kitchen was tense, and Joyce knew her presence had caused that. She had made them so uncomfortable that they were momentarily dumb.

She grabbed a can of soda and moved back toward where she'd come from.

"Joyce, honey." She heard her father call.

She turned slowly to regard him, hips cocked to the side. Emily had pushed away from him and was now maintaining an appropriate distance. "We should talk."

She laughed mirthlessly. "I don't see that there's anything more to talk about. Or do you?" She asked, directing her question to Emily, who seemed to find the pizza box awfully interesting. "That's what I thought," she said, moving back towards her room.

Larry, she'd learned, was out. She understood he needed space to come to terms with the news in his own time. And so, she spent the rest of the evening just lounging. And for the next couple of days, she did the same thing, except that she practically only hung out with her brother. Emily, it would seem, was also moving in with them. And Joyce had had to watch her climb up to her father's room once or twice. She felt like dragging her down the stairs by her hair.

She had still not told her mother about it. No one had. Not even her father had the courage to do so. She wondered why everyone was afraid of breaking the news to her. She had wondered why. How badly were her mother's feelings going to be hurt? Seeing that she hadn't had any answers to those questions, she had pushed them to the back of her mind and had tried to enjoy herself.

Larry had, surprisingly, not mentioned David. Even though Joyce was aware, they kept in touch. She had felt the urge once or twice to ask after him, platonically, of course, but hadn't wanted to send the wrong message to her ever perceptive brother.

On the afternoon of the fifth day, Joyce found herself feeling awfully hot. And so she found herself staring longingly at the pool where Emily swam, her face blissful. She tried to tell herself that the heat wouldn't kill her, but it was so sweltering that she began to sweat between her thighs.

Unable to keep away from the sight of the enticing pool anymore, Joyce stripped out of her faded jeans and tank top and pulled on the bikini she had packed. She twisted her hair into a sloppy bun and quickly stepped out. She moved towards the pool area with trepidation. She was only out to catch a swim, not bond with her father's wife-to-be. Over the course of living here, albeit temporarily, she had watched the way they conversed. If she said she'd not seen how taken her father was with Emily, she'd be lying. And the woman seemed to genuinely care about him.

And she had no anger or resentment to hold onto after that slow revelation. But just because she didn't want to rip her hair off did not mean she wanted to knit with her and bond over tales of old college boyfriends. But as she moved towards the edge of the pool, Emily, who'd been taking deep strokes, turned towards her and gave her a grin.

Joyce simply eyed her like she would a TITANOBOA. "The heat drove you out too?" Emily started conversationally, swimming in her direction.

Joyce's only response was a nod, and she lowered herself inside the pool. The cooling waters caused her to let out a pleasurable moan, her cheeks flushing when Emily laughed. "I feel you, sister."

She managed a low chuckle, wondering if Emily was always this naturally cheerful. The woman had been nothing short of nice, given how badly behaved Joyce had been for the past few days.

Even her mother, no matter how hurt she was, would not have approved of her behavior.

"I love the bikini," Emily said. "Where did you get that?"

Joyce turned midswim towards Emily. "You know that there's a place called the mall where humans go to---"

"Okay, I get it." Emily laughed, not the least bit offended.

Joyce nodded and continued to take laps. She was enjoying the temporary quiet and wishing Emily would continue to shut up and not try to play the nice stepmother. As Joyce swam towards the edge of the pool, she pulled up slightly to catch Emily pushing out of the pool. Her bikini looked great, even better than hers. It looked like those designer ones her uppity college girls had often worn.

Two hours later, when Joyce decided that her body had had enough, she went to one of the lounges chairs to rest, completely ignoring Emily, who was occupying one.

"You feel great, don't you?"

"Yeah," Joyce replied. Hopefully, her curt will reply would tell her off. But she wasn't that lucky.

"I love swimming."

"I can tell." The words were out of her mouth before she knew it.

Emily grinned at her. "It's a favorite hobby of mine. My parents have taught me since I was little."

"That's great," Joyce said, her shoulders beginning to burn. She couldn't begin to yell when the woman was being this friendly, and she wasn't that horrible.

"Yes." Emily turned her annoying smile at her, worry quickly taking over her features. "You've got a burn, Joyce. Did you use any sunscreen?"

As Emily asked that, she was already getting up and moving

towards her, sunscreen in hand. When she got close, Joyce tried to snatch the cup from her, but she held steady on it. "No. You can't do it yourself. You'll hurt yourself further."

Joyce conceded and allowed Emily to claim her lounge chair and apply the sunscreen. She was very careful, and her touch was soothing, kind of like her mum's. When she was done, she said, "All good!"

"Thank you."

"Anytime," she answered simply.

"So, like I said, my parents supported me when I was a kid who adamantly wanted to be a professional swimmer. I became good at it. In high school, I was the best. If I could say so myself."

"What makes you think you were?"

“Winning for three straight years made me think so.” She didn't look smug or self-absorbed. Joyce had to give her brownies for that.

As the afternoon wore on, Joyce found herself learning about Emily. She appeared to be from a well-off family based on the pieces she could gather. Another shocking revelation was how great it felt to talk to her. Emily, smartly, did not bring her father into the conversation, something she was very grateful for. As they moved into the kitchen to prepare dinner, Joyce realized that sunny Emily was beginning to win her over.

CHAPTER SEVEN

The coming days in the townhouse became a little more pleasant. Joyce had grudgingly come to accept Emily's impending union with her father. She had caught herself enjoying the woman's company. Emily was not just a cute head; she was smart and insightful, and fun. And since she was nearly as young as Joyce was, they both found themselves bonding over glasses of wine and beer at least a couple of times.

Larry had not come around to accepting the whole ordeal but had begun to be civil to Emily, giving more than one-worded replies, being politely friendly, but staying out of the woman's way as much as he could. Joyce could not help but notice that the relationship between Larry and her father was strained. She wondered, not for the first time, if it was the appearance of Emily in their father's life or if this had gone on for far longer than she would have cared to know.

Two days before her journey back to Chicago, she'd been nursing a glass of wine on the patio, feeling awfully content to be bathed in the glow of the sun as she watched its descent. Emily had joined her a while later, a glass of wine in one hand, the whole bottle in the other. Joyce had snorted at the sight but had not raised any questions. She knew her father would be flummoxed to realize that his wife-to-be and daughter had steadily razed through his stash.

She smiled evilly at the thought of having Emily explain that to get father. But of course, since she was the love of his life, there was so much she was going to get away with, including putting a dent in his wine cellar.

"What has got you smiling like that?" Emily asked as she settled herself on the chair close to hers.

Joyce tried not to squirm uncomfortably at the closeness. "Trust me, you don't want to know."

Emily wriggled her brows at her suggestively. "Were you thinking of someone, perhaps?"

Joyce turned incredulously to regard her. "God, no. What makes you think that?"

Emily's smile faltered a little. "I uh, I wasn't thinking that... I mean, I was-- not just in the way you mean."

Joyce was even more confused. "What do you even mean?"

"I didn't mean to assume you have a boyfriend or anything of the sort. I was merely teasing. I mean, your personal life is yours, and the last thing I want to do is pry--"

"Emily. Calm down lest you hyperventilate."

The woman breathed out and relaxed into her chair. "Sorry about that." Joyce nodded and reached for her glass of wine, took a generous sip, and said. "I do not have a boyfriend."

Emily nodded. "Of course. I shouldn't have assumed you do. Or have someone you're into. I hated when I was constantly teased about that. And now that I have finally met someone I fancy, I wonder how--" She paused suddenly and gave a self-deprecating chuckle. "I'd hate to saddle you with my problems. Of course, the last thing you want to hear about is your father and me."

"True," Joyce replied bluntly, seeing no need in acting coy with Emily. When a look of hurt crossed the woman's eyes, Joyce backtracked a little. Just because she didn't approve of their relationship did not mean she had to continue to be a little bitch about it. Emily had been nothing short of kind and nice to her. The least she could do was return the favour. "I mean; I'm still getting used to the whole idea. It's an easier pill to swallow now."

When Emily turned to her, eyes wide and hopeful, Joyce clenched her fist and continued. "I see the way you both are. You care for him. He cares for you too."

Emily nodded. "I really do." She slowly dropped her glass of wine on the table and leaned back, shoulder slumped. Joyce waited in silent encouragement for her to continue. Figuring that Emily needed someone to talk to. Maybe, her friends had all deserted her at the news that she was marrying a middle-aged man. While that kind of thought would have filled her with glee days ago, she was only full of pity for her. They both deserved a chance at happiness, as weird as their union was going to be.

"My dad, he..." Emily breathed out deeply and continued. "He doesn't want me to marry a man that is nearly as old as he.

They were shocked at the news. Mom too. I told them about the engagement, and they do not approve."

If it were Lilian, Joyce would have wrapped her arms around her and hugged her till she felt better. But she hadn't established that sort of bond with Emily and so resorted to placing a comforting hand on her lap. "It's going to be alright."

"I don't think so." Emily quietly said, her voice low and sad.

"Why? Are you afraid your own parents would disown you?"

Emily looked up at her, eyes dark and sorrowful. "It could come to that." She looked down at her hands and said. "They wanted me to marry a senator's son who'd shown interest. They still feel I have a chance with him. A chance to right my mistake, they said."

Wow. A senator's son? Emily's parents were really up there. It finally put Joyce's fears to rest about Emily clinging onto her father's arm for his money. If her family did not approve, even with how loaded her father was...

"You do not have feelings for this other man, do you?"

"God, never. I've never fancied him. I think--" Emily said, looking a bit shy, a blush coating her cheeks. "I think I've always been attracted to older men."

"Wow."

Emily looked quickly at her. "I hope you're not weirded out."

Joyce shook her head. "You like what you like. You love who you love. You should never apologize for who you are."

Emily looked grateful. "Thank you. I think I really needed that."

"You're welcome."

Emily nodded and looked more relaxed when she grabbed her glass of wine and took a healthy sip. "This is great," she said, smacking her lips.

Joyce nodded. "It's a classic." She felt buzzed. She was not drunk. She was sure on her way to getting tipsy. Father was working late again. Larry was out, and Joyce doubted he'd be back.

"So, really? No boyfriend? You're really pretty, and I can't believe that you do not have men falling at your feet and begging to take you on dates."

“I'm pretty, and so are like, the rest of the girls on campus.” Joyce knew she was inadvertently comparing herself to other girls and didn't want to analyze what that said about her self-esteem.

Emily just looked at her curiously so that Joyce found herself saying. "I'm not much for relationships. Tying myself down to one dic-" I mean, one person has never appealed to me.

Emily nodded as if she understood. "So, I get down with men I find attractive." Her mind spiraled to her first night in California. The night she'd spent getting fucked six ways from Sunday. She tried to repress the memory, unsure it was the appropriate time to think about her one-night stand with David. But oh, hadn't it felt wonderful?

"What has got you smiling like that?" Emily asked, her eyes narrowed suspiciously at her.

Joyce could feel herself blush. "Um, I just r-remembered something."

"Something or someone?"

"Um, maybe a little bit of both?"

Emily grinned and angled her chair towards hers. "Tell me."

"It's nothing. It's simply someone I met on my first night here."

Emily's eyes widened. "You went on a date your first day here?"

"Not a date. I told you I don't do those. At least not now. It was one-time stuff."

Emily nodded, and Joyce hoped she wasn't going to try to hound for details. Emily, fortunately, did not, and they talked about other stuff. Emily was a good companion, and Joyce found herself laughing at her sense of humour and talented way of retelling stories. Two hours later, Joyce was trying to stifle a yawn.

"You'd better sleep. That's like the third time you've yawned."

Joyce laughed. "Sorry. I'm just really tired, and the drink has gotten to my head."

"No problem. I'll wait out here a little while." For your father. Even though Emily did not add that, Joyce knew it was the only reason Emily was going to continue to sit out here when she went to bed.

"Well, have a nice time waiting for his return..."

Emily gasped. "How did you--"

"He's my father, Emily. Trust me, I know him."

Emily nodded. "I guess you do. I'm just-- when he comes back so late sometimes, I worry."

"Don't worry. He will be home safe." Joyce found herself comforting Emily again for the second time that night. Was this going to become a thing?

"Thank you, Joyce," Emily said again.

Joyce nodded and made to pick up her glass of wine. But Emily halted her. "Don't worry. I've got it."

Joyce nodded gratefully and moved to her room. As she snuggled into her warm fluffy blanket, she realized that she was going to miss Emily. What a horrible twist.

*****

Joyce spent her last day in California outdoors, with Emily, of course. They visited a quaint restaurant, did a little bit of window shopping, and had an impromptu picnic. The weather was great, and Joyce was happy.

That night, her father sought her out, shoulders tensed. But Joyce gave him a genuine smile for the first time in two weeks, watching as a look of utter relief crossed his features. Had he been afraid she was going to pick another fight?

"You know; you can stay further if you wish to. I hear you have been bonding well with my--" he coughed awkwardly. "With uh, Emily."

"Yes," Joyce answered, watching him carefully. "She's been great company."

Her father nodded with a smile. "Emily is great." He looked like he wanted to say more but decided to leave it at that.

"Even if she's young, I can see why you're taken with her. She's got a huge heart." Her mind went back to the events of the afternoon and the cute hat Emily had bought her despite the fact that Joyce had tried to protest. Emily really did have a huge heart.

" You know; it'll mean the world to me if I get your approval. And that of your brother. Your mom too. I don't want to go into this knowing that the people I care about the most--"

"You care about me?"

Her father nodded. "Surely, you must know that?"

"For a while, no." Her father frowned at her. "You didn't do a good job of showing it." She added.

"I understand. But honey, your mother and I had an agreement."

"An agreement you stuck to, despite caring about me? Was it that easy? To forget me?" Joyce hadn't meant to bring all of this up, but the ugly feelings had twitched alive in her stomach, making her feel nauseated.

"I'm sorry. I felt it was better that way." I..." he breathed out deeply. I do not plan to have children with Emily."

Joyce balked at the news. "Dad, that woman practically wears her heart on her sleeve. She would want kids."

"She knows my stand on it." Her father blushed and looked down. I had a vasectomy a year after your mum and I... Joyce gasped. Her father, not looking at her, bravely continued. "I don't think I deserve to have more kids. Not when I couldn't love the ones I did right."

Joyce laughed with tears in her eyes and flung her arms around her father. "It's alright. Emily is good for you. You both have my blessings." Her father clutched at her and hugged her right back. He may not have been the best father in the world, but he loved her. He did, and for now, that was all that mattered.

CHAPTER EIGHT

The following month proved to be very difficult for Joyce, who nearly ran herself to the ground studying for her last papers, turning in assignments, and generally trying to ensure that she graduated with a decent enough grade.
It didn't help that she constantly had to fight off nausea and headaches. One too many times, she had found herself falling asleep while she studied. Even though it was something that generally occurred to humans, she was still appalled at herself.

And then, despite the constant stress, she began to gain weight. She broke out terribly and constantly craved frozen peas. It was the weirdest, weirdest period of her life, which she attributed to her last days on campus. Even Lillian had become withdrawn and more focused on her books. They were all trying to get out with a decent enough GPA to land them a good enough job out there in the real world. It was no big deal. Once she went up on that large podium to get her certificate, all of this was going to end.

The thought got her through her last paper, and three months later, Joyce was walking up the podium, all smiles, to receive her certificate. As she beamed at the crowd, her eyes landed on her family in the crowded room. Her father wore a proud smile, and so did her mum. Larry was grinning, but David, who'd appeared to accompany Larry, had a bland look on his face.

Over the years, her parents had come to some sort of truce and had even attempted to be light friends. Their divorce had not been dirty and drawn out or anything like that, which was something she was eternally grateful for. And so, seeing all of them in one of the rows, watching her with matching grin, caused her to imagine that they were a true family once again and that nothing had changed.

As she walked back to her stand, she felt a bit dizzy. Attributing it to the buzz and thrill of the day, she hurried to her seat. The rest of the ceremony continued and ended without a hitch. Two hours later, Joyce ran out to the parking lot to find her family huddled together, waiting for her. As Joyce looked between her father, Emily, and mom, she wondered if her mom knew. There was an engagement ring on Emily's hand. Surely, her mother must have noticed that?

She watched her mom closely, but there was no sign of distress. Her eyes were bright, and her smile was genuine. She even seemed not to take notice of Emily and her dad, who stood a bit awkwardly to the side. As she moved toward them, she opened her arms in a hug, and Joyce fell right in. "I'm so proud of you, baby." She crooned.

"Thank you, mom."

"Congratulations, little sister," Larry said. Joyce gave him a mocking glare, blinking when another dizzy spell happened.

"Are you alright?" She heard Emily ask. She turned towards her and tried to give her best convincing smile. "I'm more than okay."

"It's just, you look a little pale," Emily said, biting her lips in worry.

When her mother turned a concerned gaze on her, Joyce waved their worry away. "I'm perfectly okay. It's the frenzy of the day."

"We should all get lunch. And you should get food in your system too, young lady." It was her father. He had a little smile curving his lips, and Joyce was flat grateful that everyone was getting along. It meant a lot that they'd all put their feelings aside and decided to be civil to each other on her big day.

Joyce nodded at her father. "Lunch sounds great. I s-should go say hi to Lilian's paren-" the world tittered around her and then, a second later, faded to black. As she slipped into unconsciousness, she felt arms wrap around her, worried voices. A shout. A scream. And then, nothing.

******

Joyce woke up to the sound of beeping. Her eyes felt like granite had been heaped on them, her tongue felt heavy and swollen, and she found it impossible to swallow. Five minutes later, when she could finally crack an eye open, she realized she was in a bed, not just any bed, a hospital bed. The walls were white, and the room smelled funny.

Wrinkling her nose, Joyce tried to get up.

"I wouldn't do that if I were you." It was a feminine voice she had come to know. Emily. There was shuffling of feet, and a moment later, the side of the bed dipped. A soft hand was placed on her arm that wasn't connected to some sort of drip. "How are you feeling?"

"Like a truck ran over me." Emily chuckled at her dry reply.

"Where are my parents?" She asked.

Emily worried her lower lips; an act Joyce was beginning to realize was a habit. "Your father left."

"Oh," Joyce muttered. She wondered what she had expected. To find him sleeping in one of these uncomfortable chairs, looking like he was at death's door himself?

"Joyce, when you slumped at the parking lot, your dad neatly suffered a heart attack. When we brought you here, the doctor advised him to go home to rest. It was obvious that seeing you like this nearly did him in."

Joyce nodded. "And my mom?" She asked.

"Larry took her to the hospital cafe. They should be back any second."

"Are you sure you're feeling alright? I should call your mother, and of course your father too. They need to know you're awake. B-but of course, I do not have your mother's contact information, so I'd just have to call your dad." She whipped out her phone and began, took it to her ear, and stepped away.

Less than twenty minutes later, Joyce's hospital room was filled with concerned faces. The doctor had been called. Her mother had practically not left her side, and as Joyce gazed at her, she swore she could see tear streaks. Her heart clenched at the sight.

The doctor asked her a series of questions and then checked her vitals. When he was certain that everything was in order, he sat gingerly on the edge of her bed. Checked her chart again (probably to remember her name or something) and then looked at her. "How are you feeling, Joyce?"

"Tired." She managed in a croaky voice. Turning towards the doctor, she asked. "Can I have some water?"

"Certainly." He said, making to ring for a nurse. But her mother held up her hand and was beside her bed in a flash, gingerly helping her take slow sips of water.

"So, we ran physical tests on you while you were unconscious because you needed to determine the cause of your fainting spell." The doctor spoke in a cultured professional tone.

Her mother turned towards him worriedly. "What was the diagnosis, doctor?"

But the doctor, offering her a bland smile, looked toward her. "Would you like to have the results read here, or would you rather I talked to you personally first?" The doctor was giving her an out, and it was obvious in the way he looked straight at her that whatever he had discovered was pretty much serious.

Fear engulfed her like a woolen cloak, and her hands shook. At this point, she was on the verge of fainting again. What could possibly be wrong with her? Was it some sort of deadly disease with no cure? At the knowledge that she could have cancer so early in life, tears clogged her eyes.

The doctor, sensing her distress, laid a placating hand on her arm. "It's fine. Would you like this to be a one-on-one?" It was apparent that the doctor could shepherd her parents out of the room if she wished it. But this sort of news was something she'd need their support for. "I'm okay with them listening in." She said, offering the doctor a brave smile.

"Alright. It seems that you are pregnant. While we haven't done a conclusive test to decide--"

"She's what?"

"I'm what?" Mum and I spoke at the same time, my eyes were wider than saucers, and I could feel myself hyperventilating.

"You're very wrong. Doctor. I have been seeing my period, and it's been very regular, thick as always--" She saw her mom wince and decided to shut up.

"Joyce," the doctor said in a tone that brooked no arguments. "I conduct physical examinations on patients all the time. I'm afraid my conclusions are spot on. It would seem you're three months gone already, but we can still conduct a medical examination--"

"Yes, please," Joyce said, making to get up. The doctor was very wrong. He had to be. Her period had been regular, but even as she tried to convince herself of this, her heart pounded so hard she was afraid it'd pound right out of her chest. Something was niggling at the back of her mind. The strange symptoms she'd been having and the night with David... Fuck! But the doctor could still be wrong. Right?

Three hours later, after Joyce had wrung her hands out of worry. A nurse came back with the test results. Her family had all waited with her. Emily had had to leave. So, it'd just been Larry, David, and her parents. Larry could not even look her in the eye, and she was filled with utter shame so much that she too could not look her father in the eye.

She took the test result with shaky fingers. The nurse's expression gave nothing away. When she looked down at it, her heart came to a screeching halt. She felt more than saw someone peer at the sheet over her shoulders. And a moment later, a shaky voice said... "Oh my God." It was her mother, and she looked like she was the next in line to faint.

"Who did this? Who did this to you?" Her brother asked, coming closer to her. His eyes were hard, and his lips had thinned into an angry line. "Tell me!" He growled.

"I don't know." She cried. "I don't e-even, I-I t-thought it was s-safe--" her lips quivered so badly she couldn't quite get the words out. Everything felt like a dream, and for a split second, she was tempted to pinch herself to be sure that everything that had, in fact, happened was real.

"What do you mean you don't know?" Her father roared. "Tell me who fucking did this."

When she looked up straight at David, he was staring at her with panicked eyes. "Tell me this second."

With trembling fear, she pointed at David. And after that, everything happened like she was in some sort of multiverse. Larry lunged at David, delivering a blow to his jaw that caused her to cry out. "You stupid piece of shit, I trusted you!" Another punch. David didn't even try to defend himself. One of the nurses must have informed security because they stomped into the room just in time to drag Larry off of David, who had begun to bruise.

"I'm going to fucking kill you." Larry howled, struggling in the burly man's grip to get back to David and finish him for good. The doctor turned to her, and she saw something that looked like sympathy in his eyes. He managed, five minutes later, to usher her and her parents to his office, where he talked to them in a calm, professional voice.

Fifteen minutes later, the doctor ushered her parents out of the office and came back to his desk to regard her. They were silent for several minutes until Joyce found herself saying. "I didn't know. I thought it was my s-safe period. I-I--" but the doctor forestalled her.

"I'm sorry you had to find out this way, but I've been in practice long enough to see similar cases. Your pregnancy is mildly cryptic. We will know for sure as it progresses. And, of course, you should know there is no safe period for a woman. The idea that a woman is safe a couple of days after her period is just crap. You're only completely safe when you're on contraceptives or your partner uses a condom."

Joyce nodded, tears filling her eyes. David had not used a condom that night. The sex had happened in a frenzy. They hadn't wanted to be caught. For the first time since it happened, Joyce wished she had torn her head out of the nest of lust long enough to insist on a condom. Or hadn't been too caught up in the little family drama to forget to take a morning pill. But the milk had been spilled, and she felt hollow inside. So completely hollow, she wondered what the heck was happening from there.

CHAPTER NINE

The next hour passed in a blur. Joyce could remember the doctor talking about referring her to a gynecologist and giving her a card of some sort. She left the hospital in a daze. The car ride was filled with so much tension she was at risk of getting suffocated. Her mother, who still had tear streaks on her cheeks, looked robotically at the road ahead, refusing to glance her way or start any form of conversation.

After the events of the day, she understood they needed time to process, as did she. She looked out the window, still in a state of disbelief that this had happened. She was having a baby? She? A girl in her twenties who had only hours ago graduated college? What were her friends going to think? Oh, God.

She moved her hands to her stomach, cradling it softly, still finding it almost impossible to believe that there was a baby growing in there. The doctor had said her pregnancy was mildly cryptic, which pointed to why she hadn't even known she was having a child in the first instance. She shook her head softly at herself, berating herself for having been so careless. Her mind went back to David, the man who was responsible for all these. Why hadn't he used protection? Even as she thought about it, she knew she could not blame him. It was her responsibility to keep herself safe.

With fresh tears in her eyes, she leaned against the car window and closed her eyes. She opened her eyes to a light tapping on her shoulder. They'd arrived home. Her mom was looking at her concernedly. "Are you alright?" She asked. "You should eat something. Let's go in."

When she looked out the window, she realized they'd arrived home. Her mum led her to the kitchen with a soft hand on her shoulder, which she found oddly comforting. "Your dad would be having dinner with us," she said.

Joyce quietly nodded. "That guy will be here too."

"Who?" She asked softly.

"The guy who... What's his name?" Her mother said as if she could not bear to call him by his name.

Joyce nodded again. It seemed like she'd been doing an awful lot of that lately.

That evening, dinner was a tense affair, giving her a strong sense of Deja Vu. As her father bit into his orzo, he declared acidly. "Joyce, you will live with David until you deliver."

Joyce opened her mouth to protest, but Larry's glare silenced her. David ate quietly with as much dignity as he could muster. Joyce had found it difficult to look in his eyes. And had looked at everywhere but at him. Her father continued, tone hard. "He has accepted full responsibility and would care for you until you give birth. When the baby is born, you both will co-parent. He will pay for child support, of course..."

"Dad," Joyce said, voice hollow and shaky. "Why force David into this? I can work and care for my own child."

"But you won't, her father cut in evenly. Not even the one who put you in the family way is walking about with his testicles hanging free."

Joyce fought a blush at her father's callous words and looked right back to her orzo, which was quickly getting cold.

"Eat," Joyce. Her mother, who had been watching her play with her food, ordered. "We will pack today. And tomorrow, you go to David's."

"But he's living with Larry. Joyce still attempted to protest. How will we manage that?" She couldn't imagine an environment with David and Larry. Judging from the way Larry glared at his friend, he wasn't forgiven.

"Not anymore." It was Larry this time.

Joyce nodded, forced spoonfuls of the orzo down her throat, and completely surrendered herself to her fate.

*****

When Joyce arrived in California, Larry's room had been cleaned out of all his personal belongings except the bed and other important household items she would need. She'd driven back with her mum, who had helped her unpack. She wondered how this was going to work. Everything seemed so sudden. It was a whirlwind, and not for the first time, she fervently hoped she was in some sort of trance she would wake up from.

Her mother had brought everything she would need and had even managed to pack her a few maternity gowns. Cringe. She couldn't believe that in less than seven months, she was going to be a mother. Was that a role she was ready for? She shook her head softly, looking up when her mother placed a hand on her shoulder. “Everything will be fine, honey.”

She smiled at her gratefully. Her mom had absorbed the news, processed it, and was now supporting her fully. She rose and fell into her arms. "I'm sorry." She whispered.

"It's alright." Her mum said. "I'll be a grandmother soon. It's something I'm happy about."

"B-but I di--"

"Shhhh." Her mum said, placing her finger against her lips. "Don't condemn yourself. We all make mistakes. But I have a good feeling about all this. Stop feeling bad about it, okay?"

She nodded. She felt very grateful that her mother was not as disappointed in her as she thought she would be. "Now, I have to hurry back to meet up with my morning shift." Joyce nodded and walked her mum to the door. When she came back, she moved towards David's door, more out of curiosity than anything else. But realized she couldn't bring herself to open the door. Didn't want to be plagued with the memory of that night

But she gasped when the door swung open, and she came face to face with David. He had ice against the side of his jaw and leaned one shoulder against his door, and regarded her silently. She didn't know what to say. After several tensed seconds, David finally spoke. "We should talk."

"We should."

"Let's go to the kitchen." He said.

They moved to the kitchen together. She sat gingerly on one of the chairs. David turned to her. "Should I pour you something? A glass of wine, perhaps?"

She frowned at him. "Wine? In what universe are pregnant women advised to drink wine?"

David simply glared at her, turned towards the fridge, and poured her a glass of juice. Dropping it on the island with slight force.

"Maybe you should begin to read up on pregnancy so that you won't offer me god awful shit."

"You sound like you aren't dying to drink it."

"I'm not." She all but growled, annoyed that he was so right. Even though alcohol during pregnancy was simply unacceptable, she found that she craved it even more than usual.

"Why didn't you tell me?" David asked.

"Tell you what?"

"That you were not on any contraceptive. That you know next to nothing about avoiding situations like this."

"Why didn't you tell me you don't know how to use a condom?" She retorted, eyes flashing.

"This is stupid." He said, moving away from the kitchen.

"Come back here. We aren't done."

"I am."

"No, you're not."

"Yes, I am. I'll take care of you as I have assured your father. You will give birth to this baby, and you will be out of my house. Right now, six months feels like six years. What the fuck." He growled as if he couldn't believe this had happened.

" The fuck, you will just boot me out as soon as I pop this child. We are going to behave like adults, talk this out and try to come up with a plausible plan."

" Okay. Humour me." He said, pushing his bedroom door open and going in. Joyce found herself moving into the room with him as she spoke. "First, you start to read. I can't be the one learning all this strange stuff on my own." She ticked off each point with her finger. "Second, we begin to buy baby things. Third, we find me a--"

her voice petered out when her eyes trailed towards the bed.

She felt a blush coating her cheeks, and this time, she could not fight it. Her neck reddened, and she tried to resume where she'd left off but realized she had completely lost her train of thought. Right there on that bed was where she'd had the best sex of her life. The events of that night thundered through her until she could remember every groan and whimper. Every word, uttered through feverish lips.

"Um, maybe we should continue this conversation in the living room." She said.

"Why are you so red?" He asked, a little bit of worry in his tone. "Are fainting spells going to be a regular occurrence?"

"No." She snapped. And this time, she pulled her eyes away from the bed and moved towards the living room, glad when David silently followed.

"And I have to find a gynecologist."

"That can be arranged."

"What should I expect?" He asked. "I've never been around a pregnant woman." He was eyeing her stomach, which was still flat, by the way.

"How should I know? You gotta start reading. Apparently, this is almost the end of my first trimester."

"Oh," David said.

"Yes." She answered. "We will learn as we go, I guess."

" Um, yeah."

"Look," he said after another minute of tensed silence. "I'm a player. And er, even though marriage and stuff like this isn't exactly a problem, I'd like for us to keep this on the low, away from the media. My agent says this could be bad publicity. And bad publicity only does good for actresses, not footballers like us."

" So, you want to keep me a secret?" She asked, hurt coursing through her.

" No, Joyce. You're not going to be my dirty little secret. We just have to keep this under wraps, and it's only temporal. There's a famous club I'm to be signed with, and until that happens, I don't think the media should get wind of this."

"No problem," she said. Swallowing a ball of hurt. Thinking quickly, she said. "I am not being referred to as your baby mama or whatever ludicrous tag there is. And we aren't in a relationship. So, I can afford to go on dates."

"With the pregnancy?" David balked, eyes throwing off sparks. "You won't take my baby on any bloody date with some guy." He announced, looking so mad she nearly chuckled evilly. Payback's a bitch.

"So, what? I'd remain here like some sort of nun?"

"Why? Is there something you might be implying? Have there been more men after me? Huh, Joyce?"

She stared at him in disbelief. "How can you even ask that?"

"Well, your stupid innuendo brought this on."

"You are the only bloody guy I've been with this year. You bloody piece of sh-" She gasped when she realized that she was sprawled on the couch, David half on top of her, hands covering her mouth.

"I hate how sharp your tongue is," he muttered, his minty breath fanning her cheeks. "And you should stop cursing like an ugly sailor. Don't make my kid grow up with that sort of barbaric attitude. You said it yourself; we are about to become parents. Better we start now to act like it." Joyce only half heard what he said, and her body was suddenly filled with so heat, heat she was sure spooked from his body.

Her nipples were painfully aware of the slight pressure on them from where his arms crossed towards her lips. She could feel her nipples beginning to harden and the all too familiar feelings of arousal flowing through her veins. Her eyes fluttered closed as her nipples tightened further until she found the wherewithal to push his hands off her mouth. "I've bl--, I uh, I've heard. Can you get off me now?" Her voice shook slightly, and she wondered why.

When David slowly lifted off of her, she noticed the way his eyes shifted quickly to her lips and away. She sat up slowly and winced when her blouse grazed her nipples, making their puckering noticeable through her shirt, something she realized with a blush that David had noticed. Damn! It was going to be a torturous six months.

CHAPTER TEN

David was awoken by the clanking of utensils and a croaky voice that belted out a Miley Cyrus song he could not pinpoint. The high pitch sounded like a howl, and for a moment, David worried she was in danger. Because, of course, it could only be one person who'd forced him awake at the crack of dawn with such a singing voice.

Joyce

He sighed, fluffed his pillow, and tried to catch a little bit more shut-eye, something that became impossible with the continuous belting tone from the kitchen. Growling under his breath, David roused out of bed and moved to the bathroom to do his ablutions. Even though Joyce had been living in his apartment for a week, it was still a bit difficult to believe they were in this situation. Sometimes, he waited with bated breath, expecting someone to pop out of thin air and tell him this was all a stupid joke. But so far, none of that had happened.

The more time Joyce spent here, the better he realized how real this was. In six months, he was going to be a father. He'd regretted that night of rendezvous with every fiber of his being. Joyce had been a tempting little demon that night, and he'd found himself succumbing to his basal desires. Looking back at it, he wished he'd simply controlled the urge to fuck her and simply...take matters into his own hands. Literally.

Sometimes, when they had dinner or lunch together in the kitchen, as they often did, David found himself watching her, trying to repress the feelings of lust that had begun to rear its ugly head. Again. He couldn't deny the fact that Joyce was a beautiful thing. Her coffee brown eyes fascinated him. Her plump, soft lips constantly beckoned to him, a call he had bravely refused to answer. He was going to keep his hands and lips off the woman, even if it killed him.

With a groan, he slipped out of bed, knowing that lazing in it was going to invite even more thoughts of the woman who was rummaging around in his kitchen. He walked into the kitchen, his skin prickling at the sight of the mess. What the hell was this woman trying to do? Create a nuclear bomb?

"What the hell are you doing?" He asked. They'd settled into a nice routine for the past one week. Joyce had found a suitable gynecologist. And had bought and dumped half a dozen books on his laps four nights ago. And, of course, that night, he'd begun to read them, his eyes widening with every description of the urethra and embryo until his head had swum.

"What does it look like?" She retorted. They'd been like this for the past week. Always arguing until one of them became too exhausted to give another vicious come back. The woman's pregnancy had already complicated his life, but her messy lifestyle was going to be his ruin. He winced at the dirty plates in the sink.

"How many times do I have to tell you?" He growled. "Clean after yourself."

"And how many times do I have to tell you that I hate to be bossed around?"

"Telling you to act like the adult you are means I'm bossing you around?"

"Who tells an adult when to wash their own fucking plates?"

"I do!" He found himself yelling. It was barely 8 am, but his head had already begun to throb. They'd constantly argued about a lot of things for the past week, but never this early. Remind him never to get married!

"Because you're what? My fucking father?" Her eyes flashed with anger, and David found himself enthralled at the sight. No, no, no. The sight of the woman's anger wasn't appealing. Nothing about her was. Except for the way her cute short pyjamas exposed toned legs. She was wearing a tank top that molded itself against the curve of her body, emphasizing her stomach that was still flat but without the slight abs, he'd imagined tracing his tongue against that night.

Fuck...

"Your father would tell you the same thing I just did." He said, feeling triumphant with her eyes widened. He was right.

"Fuck you!" She yelled and began to stalk out of the room.

"You did once." He found himself saying

His words, which he'd uttered without thinking, caused her to halt in her tracks. "What did you say?" She asked, turning to face him. He watched her, noticing the pulse on her throat, which hammered so hard he could see it all the way from here. Was she furious? Or was it something else...?

"Clean your plates. Do not leave the remote on the couch after you've seen the movie. The list goes on and on, Joyce. These things are simple life habits adults like us imbibe to make our own lives better."

She simply whirled around and stomped out of the room, leaving David to clean the mess in the kitchen. Because he couldn't bear to see the sight of it. It irked him. Larry had often accused him of having OCD, but not even he was as messy as his younger sister.

He decided to pick up where Joyce had left off and completed her lazy attempt at making coffee. The kitchen was clean and sparkly, just how he liked it. After another minute of sipping his coffee alone, he grabbed a mug he'd mentally begun to refer to as Joyce's, poured her some, and took it to her room. When he knocked, she said. "Go away."

"With this cup of coffee?" He was smiling but didn't care to analyze why.

Her voice was filled with indignation that even he heard with the door between them. "A pregnant woman--"

"Isn't supposed to have more than two cups of coffee a day. He cut on smoothly. Come on, I Googled it."

After another agonizing minute of staring awkwardly at her door, she emerged. And this time had on spandex shorts. His eyes moved surreptitiously over her body, his brain coming to a screeching halt when he noticed that she was, in fact, not wearing a bra and her breasts were bigger and rounder than he remembered. Of course, the book had mentioned it was normal for pregnant women--

"I'm trying to restrain myself," she said, moving forward to get the coffee, sipping it instantly and releasing a sigh. "This is good."

"I'm pretty good at whatever I set my mind to do." He blurted without thinking, his heart hammering when Joyce's eyes widened, and a furious blush coated her cheeks and neck.

"T-that you are-ah... I mean, of course."

Valiantly ignoring all the possible other connotations his words had implied, he said. "I'll be leaving for practice in an hour."

She nodded. "You should eat something. Never practice on an empty stomach."

She sounded so much like a concerned girlfriend he blinked after her as she moved towards the kitchen and began to make an omelet.

He took a seat on the kitchen island and tried not to wince at the slight mess she'd made on the flat surface of the counter. She did a great job of trying to clean up, something he was immensely grateful for. After that, they settled into a comfortable silence, each digging into their own plate.

"Since we are in the habit of telling each other about our plans, I will be having a friend over." He tensed; she didn't look up from her plate.

"Who is this friend?"

"My best friend." She clarified with a frown aimed his way, which he completely ignored, welcoming the feeling of relief that coursed through his chest.

"Okay." He said

"Okay." She repeated.

!**

Lillian had arrived with a look of awe on her face. And the first thing she blurted as soon as she let her in was, "you're still flat as hell." Something that caused a laugh to burst out of her lips. Something she hadn't done in so long, laugh.

"Well, the doctor did say my pregnancy was mildly cryptic. And generally, pregnancies in their first trimester aren't always that obvious." She winced when she realized how she sounded, like an old hag. God... How had this happened?

Lillian nodded as if she completely understood. Maybe she did." So what do we have to buy? I made a list," she said, dipping her hands into her bag and producing a long-ass sheet that was filled in her neat cursive writing.

Um, Lilian," she said to her overzealous friend." The baby won't be needing all these."

" Oh. We can just strike out the unnecessary ones."

" Yes." Joyce agreed. "The baby pool will definitely have to go."

Lilian pouted. "I was looking forward to teaching our little human how to swim." Joyce smiled at the way Lilian had begun to refer to the little embryo in her stomach as human. She was grateful to be surrounded by supportive people.

"Of course, you will," Joyce said in a comforting tone.

An hour later, there were browsing through racks upon racks of baby clothes. Joyce had told Lilian about her pregnancy over the phone. She had half expected her to scream or be awkward about it. But Lilian had surprisingly taken it in good stride. Maybe it had been because she'd just finished having the most awful dinner with her parents and David in tow, which had been over a week ago. But she had found herself at the receiving end of Lilian's comforting words.

Today, Lillian could not quite manage to rein in her mischief. She's tried unsuccessfully to get her to give her explicit details on how the night had gone. But Joyce had only mentioned how great the sex was.

"It had better have been worth it, seeing as it'd pretty much knocked you up."

Despite her chagrin, Joyce blushed a deep red, which caused Lilian to chuckle loudly. "It was that great? Oh my God."

Joyce shook her head softly and grabbed a beautiful little yellow bean, silently hoping it was a girl. She'd look so cute in it. They selected more unisex clothes and, three hours later, were so exhausted they practically dragged their feet to a close-by Starbucks.

"Is this how stressful it's going to be?" Lilian questioned, heaving her leg up and massaging it slowly.

"I think we are just getting started," Joyce said, with a sigh of her own

"My God. Is it too late to withdraw my promise to be their godmother?

Joyce grinned. " You can't retract it. And of course, I'd also need me to play godmother for your little one when the time comes."

" A little wriggly baby is something I do not see in my future," Lilian said.

Joyce nodded, trying not to give her opinion on the matter. "So, are you still going to date?"

Joyce sighed. "David and I agreed to be by ourselves until the baby arrives."

"You both did what?" Lillian asked, flummoxed

"We decided it would be a great idea to er, not date."

"On what grounds? You both aren't even dating. You should be a free person, Joyce. You look gorgeous, even more so now. Your tits look great."

Thanks, Joyce said, trying not to remember the way David's eyes had drifted to her chest that morning. Had he noticed the same thing?

" Whose idea was this?" Lilian asked

"What idea?"

"This ridiculous idea of celibacy."

"David's." She answered without thinking.

"Oh..."

"What's oh?" Joyce snapped. She hadn't meant to, but talking about David and their weird pact was making her feel funny, especially at the absurdity of the whole thing. Why couldn't they date if they wanted? It wasn't like anything was going to happen between then, even if her body desperately sought for an encore.

"It sounds like the father of your child is getting possessive."

"He's not," Joyce argued. "He just... he wants this to be less messy."

"Is that what he said or what you've chosen to believe?"

"I don't know, Lilian. David hasn't given any indication that he'd like to throw me on the couch and have his way again with me."

Lilian blinked.

Joyce blushed.

"That was pretty specific," Lilian said, a teasing grin on her lips

"Um, I uh-"

"Oh, dear," Lilian said, dropping her legs to the ground and grabbing her coffee. "You've got it bad."

CHAPTER ELEVEN

Joyce and David pretty much settled into a nice routine, and as the days turned into weeks and the weeks into months, Joyce found the company of David comforting. Even though he was mostly boorish and loved to bottle up, she realized he had adapted to the task of cleaning up after her.

And because he hated to do laundry, which for someone with OCD was quite odd, Joyce found herself adding his laundry to her own routine. Three days ago, he'd taken her to dinner, which had seemed more like a date of some sort, something she'd refused to point out. The meal had been great, and Joyce had found herself laughing at his wry sense of humor.

That evening, as she gazed at him, she'd realized she wanted their child to have his magnetic blue eyes and not her boring brown ones. And so she had found herself telling him, seemingly lost in his endless pools of blue.

David had simply chuckled and said, all the while holding her gaze. "Trust me, your eyes are anything but boring." His words, uttered almost reverentially, had made her feel all sorts of funny. And that evening, as they'd driven in comfortable silence, Joyce had found herself dying to put her lips against his, to taste those firm lips once again. And she'd oddly found herself exercising self-restraint as they'd said good night at her door.

She'd noticed the way David's eyes had trailed over her form and could tell he wanted it too. David had wanted to kiss her. And that thought had stayed with her that night so that when she slipped beneath the covers and turned off the headlamp, her hands had wandered over her chest. She'd lazily caressed them, whimpering at the pleasurable jolts that arced through her body when she pinched her nipples. They were more sensitive.

Her fingers had traveled over her stomach, which had begun to grow, curving beautifully. She'd combed her fingers through her short curls and then had found her nub, rubbing it slowly at first, then frantically, helpless whimpers escaping her lips. She continued the motion until her orgasm came, pushing her slowly over the edge. She'd laid there, staring up at the ceiling, craving more. It hadn't been the same, not like David's touch. But it'd have to suffice.

One month later, she had her first appointment with her gynecologist. She'd been frightened, afraid they'd find complications. So after her less than comfortable examination, where she was forced to wear a paper-looking hospital gown, she'd emerged, hands shaking; her doctor's eyes had given nothing away. While she'd waited for the result of her assessment, David had been invited in, and as she sat there, stiff as a stick, she felt David's hands clasp hers.

She gripped onto it for dear life, only breathing out in relief when the doctor informed them that everything was normal. That day, they'd gone home and had some sort of celebration. And as time passed, Joyce discovered that her desire to kiss David had not lessened; in fact, it had grown stronger with the amount of time they spent together and the proximity that was pure torture.

She blushed when she remembered the evening he had returned from practice, sweaty. She'd taken one look at him and tried to hold in a whimper at the way he'd quickly ripped his shirt off himself. "Fuck! I feel like I'm in a boiling pot."

Joyce had been in the living room, browsing through channels. She'd gapped at him like a fish out of water, the expanse of chest and tight muscles making her acutely aware of the pulse that had begun between her legs. "Well, maybe you should go take a shower or something." She'd all but gulped out.

"Or something?" He's teased, his eyes flashing with something she could not name. Something she refused to think too much about.

He'd simply slung the damp shirt on his shoulder and moved towards his room, taking the musky scent of his skin with him. A scent she'd realized with sickening reality, she didn't want to stop breathing in. And so, Joyce jumped to her feet before she could stop herself and ran towards him, halting him with a touch of her hand to his moist shoulder.

He turned to her with a look of surprise. "What?"

"Maybe you should not take your bath yet." She'd said, avoiding his eyes.

His shock had not been disguised when he asked, "Seriously?"

"Y-yeah."

He'd given her a look akin to worry. "Are you alright?"

She'd said "yes," shifting close to his body, breathing in the natural scent of his body deeply.

His eyes had widened. "Joyce," he'd said in a weird tone of voice, prying her hands from his shoulder. "I stink, and I need to take my bath."

"I don't want you to."

"Huh?"

"I mean, the baby doesn't. I don't know." She said, and suddenly the thought of David thinking she was some sort of nutcase caused tears to wet her eyes. And moments later, she was bawling like her cat had died. David, too astonished, led her again to the living room, where he comforted him against his sweaty chest, a position she'd been all too happy to be in. When she'd almost fallen asleep, she heard him mutter. "Man, pregnancy is weird."

!****

"You what?" Lilian balked a week later when she visited.

Joyce, now a blushing mess, tried to hide her face in the palm of her hand. "I don't know, okay? I just loved the smell so much I couldn't bear the thought of not perceiving it again."

"Good thing he's a player." Lilian tutted.

Joyce simply rolled her eyes. And unconsciously, her hands went to her stomach, which had continued to grow a gentle curve. If anyone looked closely, they'd notice the slight bump. Her tank tops weren't fitting anymore. And she'd recently had to go for her more roomy tops and sundresses.

"At least you're showing now. You look the part." Lilian Sai, as if reading her thoughts

"The part of what?"

"A typical pregnant lady. Your face is filling out too."

"Thanks for the cute observation," Joyce muttered darkly. She wondered why the words stung. Another day, she'd have laughed about it. Was it the hormones? She'd seen her body and mind go through so many changes that it was astonishing.

Apart from her weird craving, she'd found herself feeling very... needy. The latest book she read on hormonal changes in pregnant women explained that it was absolutely normal for pregnant women to get horny in their second trimester. She felt like a dog in heat and had quite found that her fingers weren't doing it for her anymore. Would it be too weird if she visited an adult store?

"Your face looks funny," Lilian said.

Joyce blushed and looked away. "What is it?" Lilian asked, concern laced in her voice. They were both sitting on the sofa, facing the TV, which was blank.

Joyce shook her head. "It's nothing."

"It's not nothing. Come on, tell me."

"It's embarrassing." She quietly confessed, willing her cheeks to stop heating

"Okay, now I am really dying to hear. Is it something naughty? Did you make out with David?" A pause. "Wait!" Lilian's eyes were practically bulging out of their sockets. "Did you both have sex again?

" God, no. Why would you even think that?"

" Because your face is redder than a tomato right now."

Joyce covered her face with her palm again. "Tell me," Lilian persuaded. "It can't be that bad."

"Trust me, it's very bad."

"Hit me."

"Okay. So, um, you know how pregnancy causes us to go through physical changes? They're hormonal upheavals too. So, I'm experiencing weird cravings a-and erm..." Joyce stuttered through her mini conversation, avoiding her friend's eyes.

"You've been craving sex?" Lilian finally guessed

"Um, yeah. And it doesn't help that when I relieve myself, David is always six feet away... Sort of."

"Oh boy..."

"Bad, right? I know."

"It isn't, actually. It's perfectly normal. What are you going to do about it?"

"Nothing." She said. Vowing she wasn't going to tell her friend about her masturbation even if she tried to pluck the words out of her mouth with a hammer.

"You can get a dildo. If you're so bent on ignoring the human dildo you live with."

"What the fuck?"

"What?" Lilian asked, unperturbed. "I see no reason why you should waste money on some toy when David would gladly take you to cloud nine and build you castles there."

Joyce's pulse hammered erratically, and she managed to hold in a grunt at the thoughts of David taking her...

"I know David wants it too. He doesn't want you to date someone else. He's taken to doing your dishes and practically acting like the ideal husband--"

"That's more than enough," Joyce said. Even though she knew that there was some measure of truth in her friend's statement. That night, when she slept, David did visit her in her dream, taking her to cloud nine over and over.

CHAPTER TWELVE

David was awoken by the sound of painful groaning. As soon as his eyes popped open, he knew something was wrong. Springing out of bed, he rushed into Joyce's room to find her kneeling by the bed, her hands cradling her now noticeable bulging belly.

Fear scalded through him briefly, making him weak in the knees. With the effort of a valiant soldier, he moved to her side and, remembering what one of those books had said, decided not to cause her panic by showing his fear. He pushed her beautiful blonde hair away from her face. "Are you alright?"

"No." She laughed through a sob. "Had she been crying?"

"What's wrong? Tell me."

"It hurts." She muttered, fresh tears rolling down her face. David had never seen her so beautiful. His heart broke at the sight, and he gathered her in his arms and moved her to his room, laid her gingerly at his bedside, and rubbed her stomach slowly. The motion seemed to lessen the pain, or maybe it made it easier to bear. But the books he'd been reading had explained this solution, and for the first time since that evening when she'd dumped the books on his lap, he felt glad he had taken the time to read them.

He continued his slow, deliberate movement of his fingers on her stomach, swallowing when her breath hitched lightly. He found himself shifting even closer, enjoying the warmth of her skin against his. He pressed his face against her nape. He wondered if she felt how perfect this was. This was where she belonged—in his bed.

The next day, as he prepared to go to bed, an odd feeling in his chest, he heard a tentative knock on his door. He opened it to Joyce's big brown eyes staring up at him. "I need to stay close in case, um--*

"' Come in," he cut in, a little too eagerly. Suddenly, the world was brighter and the bed more inviting. They'd settled in pretty much like last night, David's hands on her flawless stomach, stroking softly until they both fell into a dreamless slumber.

It became a habit, their thing, that every evening, Joyce would prep in her room and, then it was time, crawl into bed with David. On a night they'd had some stupid argument, David had watched Joyce sulk into her bedroom. With a heavy feeling in his chest, David had tried to sleep, finding that he could not. After tossing and turning for an hour and making up his mind to drag the woman to his own room, the knock had come.

"I couldn't sleep," she said, avoiding his eyes when he opened.

"Neither could I." He quietly confessed. That night, as David stroked Joyce's stomach, which had become a near addiction really, he'd been unable to resist nuzzling the skin of her neck. It had been soft, smelling of jasmine. Unable to help himself, he'd kissed the soft skin, his heart rate spiking when she let out a low moan.

Oh, fuck...

And suddenly, he'd stopped. "I'm so sorry." He'd stumbled through an apology. But Joyce had simply turned to him, her stomach nestled between them, and took his face in her hands and kissed him. It had been messy, but by far the best kiss he'd had... And as he'd surrendered himself to the feelings that coursed through his body, he'd realized how hard he'd come to care for Joyce.

Her messy habits annoyed the hell out of him, but he liked to clean up after her nonetheless, a solution he'd found out had worked quite well for them. She'd prepared his meals, and she found herself getting better and better at it. They'd silently delegated duties and inadvertently chosen chores they enjoyed.

It had been pleasant with her here. And he'd even found himself looking forward to meeting his little sunshine. As he took her bottom lips between his and sucked, he realized he'd gone past caring. He loved Joyce, with her sharp tongue and eyes that darkened when she fumed.

He wanted her. All of her. And so, with a groan, he deepened the kiss, wanting to mark her as his. Mark her so deeply that she felt it down to her toes. Her whimper undid him so much that he found himself wild, tearing at the silk night top she wore, making a button pop, or was it two?

He didn't care. Right now, all he cared about was loving Joyce like he'd dreamt of doing for the past two weeks. He wanted his mouth on hers, wanted to touch her everywhere. Wanted to please her. And so, with another moan from her, which was enough consent for him, he bent down and took her exposed nipples in his mouth.

"David." She moaned, her hands going to his hair, brushing the brown curls back. The sensation of her hands in his way was wonderful. He continued to lap at her sweet turgid nipples, her cry of pleasure nearly undoing him then and there.

When he gave it one final affectionate lick and looked up, her eyes widened. "No, please, don't stop." She cried, her back arching off the bed.

"B-but we have to be careful, the b-baby--"

"Is perfectly fine. David, please," she begged, eyes glazed, mouth slightly ajar. With a groan that sounded almost painful, David raked the bodice of her silk shirt down, touching his lips to the soft, flawless flesh he revealed. He continued further down, pausing slightly at the uprise of her belly, but the desperate canting of her hips urged him on.

He planted careful kisses atop the distended stomach, his heart suddenly warm, his fingers tingly. There was a life growing inside of her, a result of something they'd both done together. As he continued downward towards her trimmed curls, Joyce began to babble under her breath, eyes closed in ecstasy. When he took his first swipe, she moaned.

He began to show her how beautiful he thought she was. Relaying his affection and fascination with her through kisses to her slit, even strokes of his fingers in her tight entrance which propelled her into an orgasm that tore a scream out of her.

Minutes later, when she managed to catch her breath, he moved back up and gathered her in his arms again, laying soft kisses on her face. The smile she gave him when their eyes met was beautiful. She looked happy and sated. "Are you okay?" He asked, even now with her emotions displayed on her face for him to see.

"I'm more than okay. That was by far better than I'd imagined." She blushed a second later at her words, and she buried her face in his chest a bit shyly. He hadn't picked her as the shy type, but at this moment, she was adorable.

"So, you did imagine, huh?"

"More times than I can care to count." Her confession caused his shaft to twitch alive, wanting to take her with a ferocity that'd render them both limp from exhaustion. But he got his yearning under control.

"Well. That makes the two of us." He chuckled, his hands moving to her hips, caressing the soft flesh there.

"You did?" She asked, raising her head to look into his eyes. "All this while, I thought I was the only one dying of sexual frustration." She laughed and then said. "From now on, I fully expect to be cared for." At her words, she parted her legs slightly and moved her hands towards...towards... Oh fuck. His eyes widened as he gazed at the movement her hands were beginning to make.

"Are you? What, really, wh--?" Closing his eyes against the onslaught of sensations and his cock that had become so rigid it bordered on painful. He said, "you know I'd gladly help."

She laughed and said. "But I what you to watch."

He moved quicker than he ever had, rummaging through a drawer and grunting in relief when his hands closed around a sealed foil. He moved back to the bed and helped Joyce on her hands and knees, ass shot out in the air. Gloving himself quickly, he brought his hands to her entrance and began to ready her. "I plan to watch you make yourself come, Joyce, but not tonight. Tonight, you come from my fingers and cock alone." And with that, he claimed her.

*****

"The baby just kicked!" Joyce announced to David, whose eyes widened in awe.

It was the weekend, and they'd chosen to laze around watching TV shows. Joyce sat up with a groan, pushed herself towards David, and brought his hands to her stomach, and they both waited with bated breath. Just when Joyce began to shrink with disappointment, they felt the subtle thump. "Oh my God," David said, his eyes filled with so much joy and affection that Joyce's eyes wetted. "This is amazing." And then he got on one knee before her and led his head gently against her stomach, and the baby kicked again, this time harder. "Hello there, little human." David grinned with a look of love, so pure tears of happiness filled her eyes.

"You'd have known what to call him if you hadn't insisted on doing this the traditional way."

"The surprise will be pleasant. Trust me," David grinned, his hands never leaving her stomach. Their eyes met over her bulging eyes, and they both grinned. Joyce had never thought an unexpected pregnancy would bring her so much happiness, but here she was, oddly happy and content. And as she continued to gaze at the stunning enigma that was still knelt in front of her, she realized he had stolen her heart without her consent. Yes, she was completely head over heels in love with this player who'd made love to her last night until her teeth chattered. This man who looked happy to do her bidding, whether he was massaging her constantly tired feet or making her a sandwich.

A knock sounded on the door, breaking both of them out of their trance. David stood quickly, his expression becoming impassive. He moved purposefully to the door and pulled it open. Larry strolled into the apartment with a glare directed at David. When his eyes landed on her, they softened a bit. "How are you, baby sis?" Like her mother, Larry had come around eventually, and soon after she'd gotten into her third trimester, he'd resumed their old habit of face timing, and it had felt like they'd never stopped.

They'd talked about anything and everything. But the one thing they never talked about? David. It was just as if there had been an unspoken rule about it, a rule that Joyce longed to break.

"I'm fine. The baby kicked minutes before you arrived." She told him excitedly.

Larry looked at her stomach, his eyes soft. Even though he was still being a dick to David, it was obvious he had begun to develop some sort of affection for the child. "Aren't you supposed to tell its sex by now?" Larry asked.

"Yeah. But um, David doesn't want us to ruin the surprise."

Larry's glare was hard, his lips thinking unto a straight unpleasant line. He didn't say anything but looked straight ahead, refusing to comment. "Larry," Joyce said quietly, "surely you're still not mad?"

"Let's not talk about this." Larry's said, squirming uncomfortably and looking longingly at the door. Was he already regretting coming? How the hell would she make the two mulish friends reconcile?

"We have to talk about it. David is the father of my child, and whether you like it or not, he'll be in this baby's life until we, we--" Joyce fumbled for words. Until they married? Until David found someone else? "I mean, he's a constant, Larry. This cannot go on." Even their father had come around and had asked after David once or twice. What was Larry's deal?

"You won't understand, Joyce."

"Hit me." She said, borrowing Lilian's line. When Larry said nothing, Joyce said. "Come on, Larry. I understand that guys have some sort of bro code that he broke, but can't you see that I betrayed you too by shagging up with him? If you cannot forgive him, then why forgive me?"

"Why are you so bothered about this?" Larry asked, his eyes skewering her.

Joyce blushed and looked away. "Nothing okay? I don't want my baby to grow up to his uncle and father butting heads."

"They'll be no head butting--"

"Then talk to him! You both go out for drinks. Do something together."

Larry looked fiercely at her and said, "No."

"You're insufferable, Larry."

"Well, isn't that my nickname?"

Joyce smacked him on the arm and groaned, trying to get up. The moment Larry had arrived, David had, of course, gone into his room. It was awkward. She hated this. If this was going to continue, she didn't know whose side she'll take. But seeing as she was getting uncomfortable in her brother's company, the answer was obvious.

"Where are you going?" Larry asked curiously.

"To the kitchen. What would you like to drink?

"I didn't come here for drinks, Joyce."

Joyce simply rolled her eyes and continued to waddle towards the kitchen. When Larry caught up with her, they fell into the ritual of preparing sandwiches to go with their cups of coffee, which was caffeine-free for Joyce. She found herself longing to explain her current situation to Larry. If he weren't being such a jerk, he'd have understood.

"Something on your mind?" Larry asked.

Joyce simply shook her head softly. "It's not something you'd like to hear."

"Come on, tell me. I can handle anything.

Joyce raised an eyebrow at his words but decided to indulge him. "I um, I've been very happy here."

Larry paused, knife poised in the air, and regarded her. She continued anywhere. "David makes me really happy. I think I'm beginning to love him." Silly. She'd gone past beginning to, but Larry didn't need to know that.

"After he did this to you?" Larry asked.

"He didn't rape me. I did what I did that night with my senses intact. I wasn't even half drunk. If anything, I was the one who egged him on," she confessed with a blush at the memory of that night in the car.

Larry shook his head softly. "This is fucked up.

"Only if we want it to be. Can't you see the beautiful side to all these?" Joyce implored. Larry shook his head. "If you don't mind, I'd like to stop talking about it."

Joyce nodded morosely. Movement was heard at the door, and when they turned, there David stood, watching the scene in from of him. Joyce wondered if he'd heard the conversation they'd had.

But David simply pulled a bottle of water out of the fridge and moved out of the kitchen. When she turned to regard her brother, she wasn't glaring at David's retreating back but rather had a thoughtful look on his face. Joyce let out a sigh of relief. This was a start.

CHAPTER THIRTEEN

Joyce had grown so big she practically could not see her feet. Everything irritated her, and she was constantly exhausted even when she basically did nothing all day. But the more her stomach swelled, the more her love for David grew.

They still bickered, and there were days she smacked him hard. But he'd developed ways to make her sulk less. Her gynecologist had said sex was no longer on the table as the date of her delivery had continued to draw near, but she was awfully content with kissing David and snuggling against him.

Emily and her father had set a date for their wedding, of course. And Emily had visited a time or two, being all bubbly as usual. David had said her large smiles and sunny demeanor made him sick. She laughed because of how hard she could relate to those feelings.

As she looked around the spotless living room, her heart clenched with love. David had begun to spoil her rotten. She was no longer allowed near the kitchen, and doing their laundry was completely out of the question. The only activity David consented to was the daily exercise her gynecologist had recommended. And, of course, her hands between his legs on nights when his hard-on kept him from sleeping, an activity she was always all too happy to help with.

Tonight, was one of those nights. She'd worked him into a snit with deep kisses that had torn groans out of him. Since she could not get on her knees to do the very thing she wanted, she had to settle yet again to having his full hard length in her hands, stroking, rubbing, settling on a rhythm he'd begun to gyrate to, until he'd come hard in her hand. "God, you're amazing," he said, kissing her softly.

"You make me." She replied, a soft smile on her features.

"When you give birth," he began, the list in his eyes receding, "what do you plan to do?"

Joyce's heart clenched hard. Were there already discussing her imminent flight out of here already? Was that how badly David wanted her gone? She swallowed hard, looked away from him, and replied. "I um, I'll find a place to stay. I might go back to Chicago, I mean, um, I-I'll definitely go back to Chicago. They're friends I know there, companies I can apply to and get a position easily. So, yeah."

David nodded thoughtfully. "Have you ever considered living permanently here? "

It's something I've managed to think about every second for the past two months. She replied in her head. But turning to David, she regarded him with wide, vulnerable eyes. "What are you asking?" It was a whisper, uttered so softly she was almost unheard.

David swallowed. A tell-tale sign that he was just as nervous as she was. "I was thinking... We make a great pair, so I, um, I don't see any reason why you should go back to Chicago. I mean, you have a place right here with me. I'd be glad if you could say yes, to staying of course. I want to spend every waking moment with the baby."

"Just the baby?" Joyce found his nervousness really cute and couldn't help herself.

David ducked his head, and Joyce smiled. While she had been worrying her head silly, David had also been having heart palpitations about her eventual evisceration from his house, something she was beginning to realize they both did not want.

"You. With you, more than anything." He quietly added and then looked at her, all along his eyes to communicate all the things he could not.

Joyce wrapped arms around him, hugging him tightly. "I don’t want to go anywhere either, David. I love every waking moment with you. I love you." Her heart had been so warm and so full that the words had fallen out of her lips without her knowledge. When David tensed against her, she dropped her hands with alarm.

" I'm sorry, is-is it too soon?" She asked, beginning to panic. Why, her big mouth!

" No. It's not that. I just never thought someone like you could love someone like me." He admitted, drawing her once again into his arms and giving her a sound kiss.

"Good." She sighed happily, returning his kisses, deepening them. She sidled against him, struggling to get as close to him as she could. Even though her doctor had advised against sex, the feelings of lust, the ache and want that coursed through her body were too much to ignore. David chuckled softly as if he could read her thoughts and moved deft hands to her breast, palming the soft flesh in his hands. "Oh yes, please. More..." She whimpered.

"But the doctor said--"

"I don't care what the doctor said." She growled.

Another chuckle, and David moved his hands to the waistline of her panties, teasing the soft flesh there lightly. "Inside, please." She begged, looking hungry and feverish.

David, suddenly filled with an inspiration that made his head hot, said. "Trade by barter."

"What?" She asked, panting. "Want another rub?"

He grinned. "I want so much more, Joyce."

"Tell me. Anything," she whispered, "I'll give you anything." When David grazed his hands against her silk panties, he encountered her moisture. Fuck! She was more than ready.

"I want all of you. Joyce. Give me all of you. Marry me, say yes. Spend the rest of your life with me. He said all in one breath."

Joyce tensed, and David shut his eyes. Had he ruined the mood?

"Is this how you do dirty talk? Do you mean it?" She asked with wide eyes that begged for it to be true.

"I've never meant anything more." He said.

The smile she gave brightened the whole room. "A proposal in the middle of sex? How unconventional."

"I'll ask right tomorrow. What do you say?"

"I say yes today. I'll say yes tomorrow too." Her eyes filled with tears and so much love it physically hurt.

"Well," he said, his hands pushing through her damp underwear, finding her soft, giving flesh. "Let me show you how happy I plan to make you."

www.ingramcontent.com/pod-product-compliance
Lightning Source LLC
LaVergne TN
LVHW050320160826
845677LV00014B/3494

* 9 7 9 8 8 4 6 0 1 6 8 4 2 *